Mountain Yarns

*Homespun Stories
Woven From The Threads of Life*

John Kincaid

Kincaid Kountry Books
Scott Depot, West Virginia

Printed and bound in the
United States of America.

Kincaid, John
Mountain Yarns
International Standard Book Number:
0-9651707-0-5

Kincaid Kountry Books
105 Cherrywood Addition
Scott Depot, West Virginia 25560

Disclaimer

Table of Contents

♠ ♠ ♠ ♠ ♠ ♠ ♠ ♠ ♠ ♠ ♠ ♠ ♠ ♠ ♠

Introduction

♠ ♠ ♠ ♠ ♠ ♠ ♠ ♠ ♠ ♠ ♠ ♠ ♠ ♠ ♠

Almost every story in this book has a moral to it. There, you've been warned. Now you can relax, lean back, and enjoy the rest of the book.

In case you have missed my first two books, let me introduce you to a place called Loop Creek and a young friend of mine who lives there.

First of all, meet my friend. You will find that some stories in this book were written by Little Johnny. He is a ten-to-fourteen-year-old boy living in the mountains of West Virginia in the early 1960s. Little Johnny always brings an innocent and sometimes painfully honest outlook on life to his storytelling. Without his contributions and his willingness to allow me to steal his stories, this book would never have been written.

Little Johnny lives on Loop Creek which is nestled safely somewhere in the Appalachian mountains. Almost all of these stories take place there. If you have ever traveled the roads of West Virginia, you have probably been through Loop Creek and never known it. That's because, on the surface, Loop Creek doesn't appear to have much to offer — just hillsides, trees, and a few scattered houses. But if you lived on Loop Creek for a while, you would know that there is ancient magic in the surrounding mountains. This magic allows almost anything to happen, and on Loop Creek, as you'll find out, it usually does.

So come on down with me and Little Johnny to Pappy's mountainside porch. As old Pappy, another friend and fellow storyteller of mine, would say, "We're gonna sit in the swing for a spell, chew the fat for a while, and spend the evenin' listenin' to a few, good *Mountain Yarns*."

♠ ♠ ♠ ♠ ♠ ♠ ♠ ♠ ♠ ♠ ♠ ♠

The Hole Story
1960

By Little Johnny

♠ ♠ ♠ ♠ ♠ ♠ ♠ ♠ ♠ ♠ ♠ ♠ ♠

"Clarence is plum crazy."

It was late spring on Loop Creek. The deep shadows of the mountains, highlighted by an early mornin' sun, were bathed in a heavy dew. An occasional car passed by on the narrow highway in front of our house, briefly interruptin' the tranquillity on the creek. Before too long, the summer tourists would be flockin' through here on their way to quiet vacations in the mountains. The grass needed mowin', but I promised Mom I'd get to it later when the grass was dry. (Sometimes the dew was so heavy that it took two or three days for the grass to dry out.) The air was full of the smell of spring flowers. You could practically see the beans comin' up in the garden beside our porch. And Mom was practicin' amateur psychology.

"What's that, Mom?"

"I said, Clarence is plum crazy. Just look at him."

We had been watchin' Clarence, who lived across the creek from us, for about an hour. On a Saturday mornin' near the end of the school year, there wasn't much else to do. Old Clarence had come out this mornin' — the bangin' of his screen door announced his arrival — fed his chickens, gathered up a pick, shovel and wheelbarrow, and started diggin' by the side of his house.

1

I enjoyed work on Saturdays, especially when I could watch it from afar, and Clarence usually provided some great entertainment. He was always hammerin' or cuttin' or plantin'. On occasions, I'd venture across the creek to talk with him. He called me "Little Blister" because I always showed up after all the hard work was done. But I would always help him cleanup, and he'd offer me a RC or a Double Cola and a moon pie. Then we'd sit on an old tree stump or a pile of lumber and talk. He was real pleasant to talk with, but sometimes he was a bit too philosophical for me, talkin' about the importance of blacksnakes, or the spiritual aspects of carpentry. But all in all, for a grownup, he kept up a pretty good conversation, at least as long as the RC Colas and moon pies lasted.

Anyway, on this particular mornin', I thought at first he was plantin' some flowers. Then as the dirt piled up, I was sure he was diggin' up a stopped-up sewer line. But as the hole grew even larger and he went from knee deep to waist deep to chest deep, I began to wonder what this latest project was all about. Mom had little doubts.

"Clarence is plum crazy," she repeated. "Probably flipped out. I knew it would happen one of these days."

"Whataya mean, Mom?"

"He's flipped out, son. He's havin' a flashback."

"You mean like in the war — like Dad does sometimes when he gets up in the middle of the night and starts puttin' all the dishes in the floor 'cause he thinks he's still on a ship and a hurricane is comin', or when he jumps behind the couch when a car backfires goin' down the road, or — "

Mom looked at me real stern-like and I shut up. I'd forgotten that we'd been talkin' about Clarence bein' crazy, not my Dad.

"No, Johnny. Just look. What's he doin'?"

"Diggin'."

2

"And what did he do all his life?"

How was I supposed to know that? I was twelve and he was seventy. I hadn't been around all his life. In fact, at my age, I couldn't remember most of my own life.

"I don't know, Mom."

"Now don't go stupid on me, Johnny. Look at the evidence. What's he doin' over there?"

I looked real hard, thinkin' this was a trick question, but all I could see was Clarence diggin' and throwin' dirt that was pilin' up higher and higher.

"Diggin'," I said, unsure of my answer.

"Right, son! And so, if he's havin' a flashback, what did he do all his life?"

"Diggin'?" I replied, still unsure of my answer.

"Bingo! Diggin'. You see, all his life he's worked in the coal mines — diggin' — sometimes sixty, seventy hours a week. And now he's finally flipped out. Folks do that when they get older. They just flip out and think that they're twenty-five again and start doin' the things they did when they were young. Why, right now, old Clarence is over there thinkin' he's back in Peabody Number Two with a mule and a wheelbarrow minin' coal. When folks have flashbacks, they're convinced in their mind that what they're doin' is real. But we know better."

"Do you mean like Dad and his fake hurricanes with the dishes in the kitchen floor?"

Mom nearly swatted my head off with the mornin' newspaper.

"Stop talkin' about your father that way," she said.

"Are you sure Clarence is havin' flashbacks, Mom. It looks to me like he might be tryin' to fix somethin'. I mean, he doesn't look crazy. After all, he's just diggin'."

Just then, Clarence emerged from his hole, wiped his hands, waved to us, and went inside his house.

3

"See, Mom, he's not crazy."

A few minutes later Clarence came back out of the house with a miner's hard hat on. He paused at the hole, waved at us again, turned on the light on his hard hat, and disappeared into the hole.

"Where's his mine mule, Mom?"

"What?"

"I said, where's his mule?"

"You don't need a real mule when you're crazy, son."

So Clarence had flipped out. Done gone crazy. And Mom had to tell everybody. Of course that took only one phone call. That's because in those days we had a party-line phone. That's where several families share the same phone line, and you can all talk at the same time.

To know how important our party line was, you've got to know a little bit about my home "town." Loop Creek, the creek, runs for about twenty-five miles through the hills of West Virginia before emptyin' into the Kanawha River somewhere east of Charleston. Small coal towns and villages line its banks, and Loop Creek, the village, is the smallest of them. In fact, Loop Creek, the village, is no more than a wide place in the road. We have a fillin' station. That's it, folks — no post office, no grocery store, no nothin' else — just a fillin' station — and a town sign. Now, most places have a sign on both ends of town to let motorists know where they are. But we're so small that we have only one sign — right smack-dab across the road from our only fillin' station. But there's a real good political reason for us havin' only one sign.

Accordin' to Dad, years ago when the station opened up, folks got so excited about the economic boom that they decided to pick a name for the place where they lived. But they ran into a big hang-up when half the folks wanted to call the place "Loop Creek" while the other half insisted on

4

calling it "Loup Creek." That touched off one of the meanest controversies in the history of Loop Creek (the creek). Even outsiders from towns as far away as Page and Beards Fork got into the debate. There were harsh words and name-callin'. There were fights and fracases, along with threats of lawsuits and lynchings — not necessarily in that order — all over the spellin' of the name.

Dad credits Grandpa Luther for workin' out a compromise. That's why if you're comin' down the creek, you'll see a sign that reads "Welcome to Loop Creek." But if you're comin' up the creek, the other side of that same sign reads "Welcome to Loup Creek." Guess that tells you somethin' about how fiercely folks hold to their opinions around here. But it's no big deal anymore. We've all gotten use to it, and since we don't have a post office, you'll never see the name on a post card.

Anyway, here in Loup Creek (the eastbound village), if you didn't get your local gossip from the fillin' station or the preacher's wife, you got it from the party-line phone. As I said before, that was a phone where everybody could get on at the same time regardless of who the call was for. Now, you could tell if a call was for you by the number of rings. Two longs were for the Jones. Two shorts was our ring. A long and a short was for Myrtle Goode and so on. The only drawback (or advantage) was that everybody could listen to your calls, and everybody usually did. So when Mom called Esther, Clarence's sister, to tell her that Clarence had flipped out, half of Loop Creek (the creek) knew about it.

"Esther, are you sittin' down?" said Mom.

"It's Clarence, isn't it? Somethin' dreadful has happened to my poor ol' Clarence," wailed Esther.

"Well, yes and no. He's all right — I mean, he ain't hurt, but he is actin' kinda crazy. I think Doc Dailey ought

5

to come over and check him out."

Mom went on to tell Esther, along with half of Loop Creek (the westbound village), about Clarence's strange behavior and her expert diagnosis. All day long after that, the phone never stopped ringin' — two longs for the Jones, a short and a long for Myrtle, three shorts for Esther. You'd have thought the fillin' station had caught on fire.

While Mom was on the phone, I spent most of the day sittin' on the porch, watchin' Clarence bring wheelbarrow loads of dirt out his hole. I kept waitin' for the loony-farm truck to show up, but it never did. Then along about four o'clock, Clarence retired for the day. It took about an hour of phone calls for Mom to explain to everybody that the diggin' had stopped and Clarence was restin' peacefully in his tree swing. No, no, he wasn't rantin'-n-ravin'. Nope, he wasn't mindlessly swingin' his pick ax. He was just restin' quietly like any ordinary sane person.

Dad arrived home a little while later along with his farming buddies Todd-n-Wilbur. Todd-n-Wilbur were actually two people, but they worked and traveled together so much that everybody called them Todd-n-Wilbur. In fact, I'd be hard pressed to tell ya which one was Todd and which one was Wilbur. But I'm sure their families would know. Now, Dad had been at Todd-n-Wilbur's farm fixin' their tractor equipment, so they didn't know anything about the tragedy goin' on across the creek. But Mom was quick to tell them all about it.

"Think I oughta go over and check on him?" asked Todd-n-Wilbur.

"No, no," said Mom. "That might really set him off. Besides, Doc Dailey said if the diggin' continues he'd go over and check on him."

"You sure you don't want me to go over and check on him, now?" asked Todd-n-Wilbur a second time.

"No, he ain't been diggin' for a couple of hours. Maybe the worst is past."

When Todd-n-Wilbur left, Dad said to Mom, "You know, with Granny's well givin' out, we have some diggin' to do ourselves."

Mom crossed her arms. "I don't want to talk about it."

"But we've got to talk about it, Jitter. (Mom's name was Jeanette, but her nickname was Jitter.) If you want water to bathe in and cook with, we're gonna have to dig a new well. And I've been thinkin' of the perfect place for it."

Mom took a guess. "Over by the willow tree. I told you I didn't want it by the willow tree. It really should go — "

"Under the kitchen."

Mom did a double-take. "Where did you say?"

Dad repeated himself. "I said in the basement under the kitchen. I'll just dig a shaft right there in the basement, and it won't take up any room in the yard."

"John Kincaid, you are crazy. There's no way I'm gonna let you — "

"Who's doin' the work, Jitter?"

"But — "

"I said, who's doin' the work?"

Mom realized she wasn't gonna win this one — at least not on this day.

"OK," she said, "we'll talk about it in the mornin'."

She didn't know what she was sayin'. By midnight, Dad had the neatest hole about six feet across and two feet deep in the basement. So much for "talkin' about it in the mornin."

Sunday afternoon Clarence and Dad resumed their diggin', and Mom resumed her psychoanalysis of Clarence. The phone was ringin' again. All the while, you could hear Dad diggin' under the kitchen, and you could see Clarence

7

from time to time emerge from his hole with a load of dirt. Todd-n-Wilbur stopped by with more disturbin' news. Clarence had actually tunneled under his house! Someone had to stop the man before he got hurt. Todd-n-Wilbur went down and chatted with Dad for a while, admired his neat, round hole, and then went on down the road.

The whole hole incident was becomin' bizarre by my way of thinkin'. Everybody was complainin' about ol' Clarence's behavior, but no one had actually gone over and talked to him. Nobody. I resisted the temptation myself for about three days before givin' in. But it got to the point where I couldn't bear it any longer. I just had to go talk with ol' Clarence and find out what he was up to. So early one mornin', I skipped school and wandered over in Clarence's direction.

When I got there, the hole was bigger than I imagined, and sure enough, Clarence had tunneled back under his house. I could hear him back in there singin' and shovelin', shovelin' and singin'. *"I'm leavin' on that New River train / I'm leavin' on that New River train / That same old train that brought me here / I'm leavin' on that New River train."* He eventually came out of his hole, pushin' a full wheelbarrow load of dirt up the incline. He deposited it on the already huge pile of dirt in his yard.

Clarence was a tall, lanky sort of person. At first glance, he looked fragile and frail, but if you looked closely, you could see powerful muscles wrapped tightly around his skinny frame. He had managed to escape the injuries and illnesses that comes with minin' coal — injuries and illnesses that had robbed other men of their skills, strengths, and lives. But Clarence was as fit as a mine mule and could pass for a man twenty years his younger. It was a shame that his mind had failed him.

"Well, well. There's Little Blister. What are you

doin' here? The work's not finished yet."

"I just come over to visit."

"You mean you skipped school just to come over and see an old codger like me?"

"Yeah, you might put it that way."

He gave me a sly look that let me know that he knew I was lyin', but that it was OK; he'd play along like he believed me.

"How's it goin'? Can I help or anything?"

"I won't have any moon pies until I go to the fillin' station at noon. Want to come back then?"

"No, that's OK. I'll just sit here and talk with ya while ya work."

"OK," he said.

With that he turned and went back down the tunnel, leavin' me sittin' by myself on his dirt pile. About fifteen minutes later, he emerged with another load. I watched as he carefully unloaded it in just the right spot and started to reenter the tunnel. He was ignorin' me.

"Clarence," I said, "can I talk to you? I mean really talk to you?"

"Sure, son. But next time ya come a-snoopin' just say 'Hi Clarence, I'm a-snoopin.' It adds a great deal to a trustin' relationship."

He was always sayin' things like that, and I always had to think for several days to figure out what he meant.

"Look, I'm just curious about what you're doin'. In fact, everybody is curious about what you're doin'. Some folks even think you're crazy. It's not normal, Clarence, to be diggin' around under your house like this."

"Oh, really? Well, what's your Dad doin' right now? Nobody thinks he's crazy. The only difference, the way I see it, is his dirt is hidden in his basement, and my dirt is out in the open for everybody to see. That's the way the

9

world works. We only pass judgment on what we can see."

"How'd you know about Dad's well?"

"Party line. I know all about what folks are sayin', and none of it is true."

"Then you're not havin' flashbacks?"

"Nope."

"And you're not havin' hallucinations?"

"Nope."

"And you're not crazy?"

"Nope."

"Then, Clarence, why are you diggin' around your house like this?"

"I'm doin' it for the glory of God, son."

Somehow I wished he had given me another answer.

"The glory of God? Clarence, that is crazy. The glory of God?"

"Tell me, son, is your Dad really happy when he's diggin' that well?"

"Well, no, not exactly. He's been complainin' and swarpin' 'cause it's goin' slower than he thinks it should." I paused to think about it. "No, Clarence, he's not happy diggin' that well."

"Is his cousin Bob happy about fixin' his car?"

"Nope. He's complainin' and swarpin' about as much as Dad."

"Do you suppose God meant it to be that way?"

"Clarence, you lost me. You totally lost me."

"As it is written, *'It is good and proper for a man to eat and drink, and to find satisfaction in his toilsome labor under the sun during the few days of life God has given him.'* Ecclesiastes 5:18. In short, son, I enjoy doin' this. It gives me great joy and satisfaction to be workin'."

"Clarence, you got to give me a better answer than that. You're doin' this just because you like diggin'?"

10

Clarence's face got real serious, and he looked me straight in the eyes. "No, son. It gives me great satisfaction because I'm keepin' a promise — a promise I've reneged on for many a year. Now you run on to school, and when the time comes, and it will, I'll tell you more. There's just two things you have to promise me: stay off the party line and next time tell me when you're a-snoopin'."

Reluctantly, I agreed to his terms and headed down the railroad tracks for a two-mile hike to the school.

Mom gave me quite a scare when I came home that afternoon. She was rushin' around in the kitchen, packin' all the dishes away in boxes.

"Mom! Mom! Are you havin' flashbacks, too?"

She gave me that aggravated-stern-like look and brushed her hair back from her face.

"Heavens no, kid. Now come on, help me quick!"

"But Mom, what's goin' on?"

"Your Dad's gonna set off some dynamite in a minute! Seems he hit bedrock in the well, and he says —" She shook her hands around her face which was gettin' redder and redder by the second. "Oh, well, just help me quick before the whole place goes up!"

"You mean Dad's gonna blow up the house?!"

"It sure looks that way, son."

As I was scurryin' around tryin' to help Mom, I couldn't help but think about how crazy it was to be settin' off dynamite under your kitchen table. I was beginnin' to wonder if maybe Dad and Clarence were sufferin' from the same delusions.

"Five minutes!" yelled Dad from downstairs. "Five minutes and I'll be ready to set her off!"

"John Kincaid, you're not really gonna do this, are you?" Mom yelled down the stairwell.

"We need the water, Jitter," Dad called back in a calm

11

voice.

"He's really gonna do it. He's *really* gonna do it."

Mom started rubbin' her fingers through her hair.

"He's really gonna *do* it," is all she could say.

"Mom, Mom! It's OK. Dad knows what he's doin'. He ain't gonna blow up the house — I think."

The scene turned real weird after that, as if everything was goin' in slow motion. Dad was countin' down the minutes, Mom was frantically emptyin' out the kitchen of everything that could be moved, and I was — well — I was standin' in the middle of the room frozen in total confusion. What was happenin' didn't seem real.

"Two minutes! . . . One Minute! . . . Ten seconds . . . five, four, three, two, one. There she blows!"

Mom and I ran for shelter and covered our ears. But nothin' happened. We were still crouched in the hallway when Dad emerged from the basement with his sheepish-I-fooled-you-big-time-didn't-I grin on his face. He walked over to the refrigerator and pulled out a cola as if nothin' had happened.

"John Edward Kincaid, Sr.! Don't you ever do that to me again."

"What's that?" he asked, downin' a big swig of pop.

"Pretend you're blowin' up the house."

"Oh, but I ain't pretendin', Jitter. I just wanted to take a little break first."

Without thinkin', Mom threw a cup at him. It shattered against the wall. In more than a dozen dynamite blasts, that cup was the only thing that got broken (if you don't count our dog's nervous breakdown and the big crack down one side of the porch).

The followin' day when I got home from school, Clarence was sittin' on top of his dirt pile. As I got off the bus, he waved to me. It was one of those come-on-over-

and-chat waves. That's all the invitation I needed.

"Afternoon, Clarence. I come a-snoopin'.."

"Good. Good. That's much better. Come, sit down."

Clarence looked a little tired. He looked as if he was carryin' somethin' heavy around on his mind. I was at that age when I was startin' to realize that sometimes the burdens we carry around in our minds are far heavier than any burden that might be placed upon our backs.

"It's almost finished. Almost finished," Clarence said. He sounded more like he was talkin' to himself than to me. He breathed out a big sigh and slapped his thighs. "You know, boy, sometimes a man is truly blessed. It's a shame that most of the time it takes the better part of a lifetime for him to realize it."

I didn't say anything.

"Did I ever tell you about the time I was trapped in the mines?"

"Really, Clarence? Were you really trapped in a coal mine? That musta been somethin'.."

"Yep. 1932. Twenty-eight years ago. Twenty three of us. I can remember it like yesterday." Clarence's face got real serious, and he started talkin' in a low, steady voice as if I wasn't even there. "Three days and three nights in the belly of the earth. Jonah and the whale. Pitch black. Suffocatin' black. Terrifyin' black with creakin' sounds. Sounds a mountain ain't supposed to make. Made my peace with God that day. Down there. October 10th, 1932. Never been afraid since. Never. Six men came out, boy. I was one of 'em — my brother, Otis Lee, wasn't."

"So that's why you're diggin' this tunnel, isn't it, Clarence? In memory of your brother?"

"Heaven's no, boy. My brother's in heaven, walkin' the streets of glory. I'm just sorry for the route he had to take to get there. And that's why I feel so blessed right now 'cause

13

I know my path ain't gonna be so rough."

We sat in silence for a long time, watchin' the creek and breakin' up clumps of dirt with our hands.

"Like I told you before," he finally said, "I got a promise to keep."

Somehow I realized that Clarence might never tell me the whole hole story. But somehow I sensed the importance of what he was doin', even if it only made sense to him. But who was I to judge? For that matter, who was anyone to judge? If Clarence had made his peace with God, he must somehow now be makin' his peace with himself, or his brother, or somebody. But that was up to Clarence and not the community.

As we sat on the dirt pile, three cars pulled across Clarence's bridge and into his driveway. It was Doc Dailey and Esther, Todd-n-Wilbur, and Sheriff McCoy. They had finally come for Clarence. We slowly rose to our feet to meet the enemy.

"Well, well, if it ain't the vigilante squad!"

"Clarence, you stop talkin' like that. I'm a duly appointed officer of the law," said McCoy.

"Yeah, maybe Max, but you ain't the judge and jury."

"Clarence, dear, we're just here because we're concerned about you," said Esther.

"Look here," said Clarence, stretchin' out his arm and flexin' his muscle. "Strong as an ox. And look," pointin' to his head, "sharp as a pick ax." He turned as if he was gonna walk back into the hole, but stopped and winked at them.

"Want a RC Cola and moon pie?"

"Clarence," Doc Dailey said, "this isn't a game. We'd just like to talk with you a while about — about that hole you're diggin'."

"Neat lookin' little hole, ain't it?"

"Clarence, stop talkin' like that, too," said Todd-n-

14

Wilbur. "The way you're tunnelin' around, I'm just afraid the house is gonna collapse in on ya."

"Look, Todd-n-Wilbur, I've lived much of my life under a million tons of mountain. You think I'm afraid of a little house?"

"You got a permit?" challenged Sheriff McCoy.

Clarence pulled a piece of paper out of his back pocket. "Right here, Sheriff."

I was closer to Clarence than Sheriff McCoy was. Clarence was holdin' a grocery list, but apparently the bluff worked.

"Clarence, honey, please," pleaded Esther, "just let Doc take a look at ya. That's all I ask."

"No way. I've seen *Miracle on 34th Street* — that guy who thought he was Santa Claus. Well, as soon as everybody found out, he was hauled off to the loony farm."

"You don't think you're Santa Claus do ya, Clarence?" asked Doc.

"No. But when I tell you I'm Bugs Bunny, the results will be the same."

Esther almost fainted.

"Clarence Caldwell, are you tellin me you're Bugs Bunny?" said Doc with his eyes squintin' and his forehead all furrowed-up.

"No, but if I did, it would make as much sense as all of you are makin'."

Finally, Doc Dailey put on his official I'm-the-doctor-don't-argue-with-me look. "Clarence, I'm going to have to ask you to come with me. Let me check you out and if everything's OK, you can come back home."

"Why don't you vigilantes just leave old Clarence alone!" I shouted. I couldn't believe I was buttin' in on grownups. I didn't even know what the word 'vigilante' meant, but I'd heard Clarence use it and it sounded pretty

15

impressive. I did know, however, that Clarence needed protection. My outburst surprised everybody.

"Look, I don't know what Clarence is doin' anymore than the rest of ya, but I do know he's not crazy, and whatever he's doin' is very, very important."

That little speech set them back only momentarily. They heard what I said, considered it, and rejected it outright. Todd-n-Wilbur came up and grabbed Clarence by the arms. Sheriff McCoy was close behind them with a pair of handcuffs. Clarence and I were losin' the battle.

"Wait! Wait!" I cried. "If you want Clarence to die an unhappy man, then go ahead and drag him off. But before you do, I just want you to know that what Clarence is doin', he's doin' for the glory of God. That's right — the glory of God. He's been ordained and appointed to do what he's doin', and if you want the wrath of Sodom and Gomorrah to come a-rainin' down on your heads, just go ahead and drag him away!"

(The words sounded so good comin' out of my mouth that I kinda got carried away.)

They all stared at me in shock and disbelief.

"The boy's crazy, too!" whined Esther. "Clarence has done gone and infected his mind."

"Wait, wait," I said, searchin' for a way to redeem myself. "What I'm sayin' is Clarence isn't hurtin' anybody and he ain't crazy like ya think. He's got a permit to do the diggin', and what he's doin' is very important. If y'all will just give him another day or two, he'll be finished with what he's doin', then y'all will see that everything is OK."

"Yeah," said Clarence, who had been silent for a long time, "and besides, I got to dig like this 'cause I'm Bugs Bunny. Ah, what's up Doc?"

There was a mischievous glint in his eyes.

Somehow that struck everybody's funny bone, and we

all gave each other one of those how-stupid-can-people-get looks and started laughin'. Todd-n-Wilbur laughed so hard that he cried. Sheriff McCoy nearly collapsed and fell into Clarence's hole. I guess you had to be there.

"Well, OK, we'll leave you alone," said Doc. "But will you at least let me check your vital signs?"

"Only if you share a RC cola and couple of moon pies with me afterwards and then leave me alone." Just then, Clarence got that real serious look on his face again. "Look folks, I'm not crazy, and, like the boy said, what I'm doin' is very important to me. I just can't tell you right now, OK? I got everythin' shored up, and the house ain't gonna fall in on me. And like Little Johnny said, I'll be finished in a day or two."

A loud "kaboom!" came rollin' across the creek and echoed repeatedly through the valley.

"That's Kincaid over there settin' off dynamite under his kitchen sink," said Clarence dryly. "Want to go see if he's got a permit, Sheriff?"

That made Sheriff McCoy laugh some more.

"No, no, Clarence. You wasted your money on that permit. You don't need one except inside city limits in this county."

"Oh, really?" said Clarence, givin' me a sideways wink.

The laughin' spell seemed to relieve a lot of tensions, and everybody seemed agreeable to give Clarence another day or two. Doc did check his vital signs. Heart rate — 75. Blood pressure — 120 over 80. Healthy as an ox. Clarence brought out some moon pies and RC Colas, and we all sat around for about an hour in the shade by his tree swing. The whole hole incident was pretty much forgotten, and everybody left that afternoon convinced that Clarence wasn't crazy, but still wonderin' what he was up to.

The next day, Saturday, I came out of the house and

17

looked over Clarence's way. Somethin' wasn't right. At first I couldn't tell exactly what was different, but then I realized — Clarence's wheelbarrow was on top of the dirt pile. Clarence was usually neat with his work. Normally, he wouldn't have left his wheelbarrow out in the open like that. I pulled on my shoes, ran across the road, and over the bridge, stoppin' at the edge of his hole.

"Clarence? . . . Clarence? You in there?"

No answer.

"Clarence!" I called louder still, but again, there was no answer. Somethin' drew me to the tunnel entrance. I looked in and saw that the tunnel ran back about ten feet before takin' a sharp turn to the right. There was a light shinin' from around the corner, and there on the wall was a large sign that read *"Don't even think about coming in here!"* As curious as I was, I respected Clarence's privacy.

"Clarence, if you're in there answer me!" My words echoed down the tunnel, but there was no reply.

All that day I watched for Clarence to show up, but all day long his place was silent and deserted. Then about an hour after dusk, my TV watchin' was interrupted by the sound of heavy machinery. It was comin' from Clarence's place. I went out on the porch, and there in the dark I could see the lights from some type of tractor maneuverin' in his yard. It was pullin' somethin' behind it, but the night was too dark to be able to make out what was goin' on. Mom and Dad joined me on the porch.

Mom shook her head and said, "Clarence really has flipped out now. He's probably levelin' his house as we speak."

Just then the tractor's motor cut off with a "clunk!" We watched for a while as he apparently unloaded somethin' and rolled it into the tunnel. After about a half hour, the old tractor roared to life again. You could hear his wooden bridge creak terribly under the strain as the tractor crossed the creek and lumbered down the road into the night.

"Should we call Sheriff McCoy?" asked Mom.

"For heaven's sakes, Jitter, leave the poor man alone," said Dad.

We retired into the house, thinkin' that all of the excitement for the night had passed. We were mistaken. About an hour later, the whole incident repeated itself. The tractor rolled noisily into his yard, a mysterious load was deposited into the tunnel, and then back down the road he went. This repeated itself like clockwork into the night until I was too exhausted to keep up the night watch.

It was rainin' Sunday mornin', and all of the activity from the night before seemed to be no more than a dream. Did I actually see what I saw or was *I* hallucinatin' last night? I hurriedly got dressed, ate my breakfast, and scurried over to Clarence's. The tunnel entrance was now boarded up with a sign that read "KEEP OUT!" From inside the tunnel, I could hear Clarence loudly singin', *"Sixteen ton an' whataya get / another day older an' deeper in debt . . ."* I breathed a deep sigh of relief. Ol' Clarence was back in his hole.

"How ya doin', Clarence? Wanna talk?" I called.

"Not now, Little Blister, I'm real busy. Tomorrow — come back tomorrow and everything will be ready!"

"Are you goin' to church with me?"

"Not this Sunday, boy, not this Sunday."

"But — "

"No buts. You can come back tomorrow, but right now I need my privacy."

Sunday passed ever so slowly. I went to Sunday School and church, but they might as well have been talkin' to the wall. My mind was back in that hole with Clarence. The afternoon dragged on, and the sun took three days to set.

That night the racket over at Clarence's commenced again. This time it was poundin' and sawin', but again his activities were hidden by the night.

The next mornin' a new surprise awaited me. There was a sign in Clarence's yard, covered by a sheet. Clarence was standin' beside it, dressed in his very best miner's outfit.

"Yow, Clarence!" I called from my porch.

"Yow, Little Blister! You can come on over now. The work is done!"

I ran across the bridge and stood by the sign.

"Ready to open up shop?" asked Clarence.

"Ready if you are," I said, anxious to finally find out what all of this was about.

Clarence pulled on the sheet, and it fell away to reveal a sign that read in big letters: *World's Smallest Exhibition Coal Mine. Admission $1.00.* I looked at the sign, and then I looked at Clarence, who was beamin' from ear to ear, and then I looked at the sign again.

"Clarence Caldwell, you are crazy. Who's gonna pay a dollar to — "

Two cars pulled across Clarence's bridge. A load of people got out.

"Oh, Harold," I heard one woman say, "isn't this sooooooo quaint."

The cars had Ohio license plates. It was then I remembered what Dad had told me about all the crazy people from Ohio. Clarence winked at me, collected his money, and led them into the tunnel for a tour. After they left, Clarence took me on a personal tour, free of charge. The tunnel was filled with old minin' memorabilia. There were hand tools and lamps and even cars for haulin' men and coal along a little narrow-gauge track. There was even a seam of coal.

"Where'd ya get all this stuff?" I asked.

"From the old deserted mine over on Johnson Branch."

"And where'd ya get that?" I asked, referrin' to the rich seam of black coal.

"Been here all along. God put it there."

"And what about this glory of God stuff?"

"It's true. Every cent I make is goin' to the church."

"And the keepin' a promise bit?"

"Oh, that was a promise I made to myself. Long ago I promised that I'd go into business for myself. But at eighteen a young girl caught my eye."

"Dreama?"

"Yes, Dreama, rest her soul, caught my eye. And the coal mines were about the only way a young man could make a livin' back then. So to marry Dreama Sue, I went to work in the mines. Every once in a while, I'd remind myself of the promise I'd made, but I never seemed to be able to find my way clear to fulfill it." Clarence shook his head. "Funny how days turn into decades . . . Anyway, that promise has been eatin' at me recently. Wouldn't let me sleep at night. And this," he said, pointin' proudly to the tunnel, "is the fulfillin' of my promise to myself. I now have a business of my very own. Now I can sleep with myself at night."

"But, Clarence, what about all the secrecy?"

"Tell me, boy, if I had told everybody what I was really up to, what would they have done?"

"They would have carried you off to the loony farm for sure."

"I rest my case."

We emerged from the tunnel to find another Ohio couple and a family from Michigan waitin' in the driveway for another one-dollar tour.

Over the summer, Clarence did a boomin' business. The church bought new hymnals, the pastor's kids got new shoes, his wife got a new dress, and the party line started

21

gossipin' about how extravagant the preacher was livin'. Clarence took the dirt from the hole and made a miniature replica of Loop Creek in his yard, highlightin' all of the coal mines, coal camps, coal wars, and minin' disasters. It was impressive — even to those of us who lived on the creek. The followin' summer Ruth Ann, Clarence's neighbor, converted her cellar into a souvenir shop, and Homer Jones turned his barn into a wax museum.

Mom wanted Dad to advertise our well as the "World's Smallest Subterranean Lake."

Dad just said, "Jitter, go take a cold shower. There's plenty of water."

Post Script

A couple of years later, Clarence got tired of all the attention and business and closed up his exhibition coal mine. That quickly closed down Ruth Ann's souvenir shop and Homer's wax museum. Consequently, Loop Creek / Loup Creek went back to bein' a one-fillin'-station town.

On occasions, Clarence would still slip down into his tunnel by himself. Especially in the evenin', you could see the yellowish lantern glow from the entrance. From time to time, I must admit, I would slip over there to see if I could find out what he was doin'. I know that snoopin' ain't right, but Clarence would have expected me to snoop. Usually, you could hear him singin' or workin' — nothin' out of the ordinary. But other times, I could hear him talkin' like he was talkin' to his best friend. At times, I almost thought I heard someone talkin' back to him. It was on those occasions that the light from the tunnel glowed whiter and purer than anything I've ever seen. I guess my mind was playin' tricks on me . . . I think.

♠ ♠ ♠ ♠ ♠ ♠ ♠ ♠ ♠ ♠ ♠ ♠ ♠

The Book Binder

♠ ♠ ♠ ♠ ♠♠ ♠ ♠ ♠ ♠ ♠ ♠ ♠ ♠

Meredith Grant beat her palms on the steering wheel as the starter on her car droned down to a stop. Dead. Now the battery was dead. How was she ever going to catch that plane? The rain poured over her windshield as she sat contemplating her situation miles from home on a deserted country road. She wasn't even sure exactly where she was. After a week of research in the mountains on Civil War ghosts, she was going home — to catch a plane — to meet Donald in Chicago. That is, that was her plan until her engine started acting up. It had teased her for several miles, running well for a while and then sputtering and choking down as if some poison had been introduced into its system. Finally, the engine had given out completely, and she had coasted to a stop near the crest of a ridge. Thank goodness, she thought, there was a place to pull off the road on this narrow mountain pass. She looked back down the road — nothing. She looked at the road ahead to see the same sight — only mountains, trees, and water being thrown around by the storm. Now what was she to do? If she could not get back to the airport in two hours she would miss her plane — and Donald.

The rain was falling even harder now as the trees were being whipped into a frenzy. What if, she thought, one of them decided to fall? She was always worrying about things like that. In her world, danger lurked in every shadow. Sometimes it lurked in bright daylight. Cars, food, strangers

23

— all possessed their own unique demons of dangers. Her only safe havens were her books and Donald. Once again her attention shifted to the trees looming over her car. What if, she thought, looking at the towering trees, that limb . . .

A knock on the windshield startled her. Beside the car stood a man who was yelling something to her though the window, but she could not hear him for the storm. Instinctively, she reached down and locked her door. She had heard tales of lonely roads and single women — unpleasant tales.

"Need some help, ma'am?" the man finally yelled loudly enough for her to hear. She did not answer. Looking into her rearview mirror, she saw the flashing lights of a tow truck nestled close to her bumper.

"What?" she said in reply.

"I said, do you need any help? There's a garage just down the road — about a mile."

What a turn of luck, she thought. Perhaps the trouble was something simple like a spark plug wire. Perhaps it could be fixed quickly, and she could catch her plane after all.

"Yes, yes. The car won't run."

"Don't worry, ma'am. We'll fix ya right up. You just stay put and lock your doors."

As the storm raged on, the man swiftly hitched her car to the tow truck. Within minutes, she and the car were deposited safe and dry in the service bay of "Elmer's Service Station." The man unhitched the car, parked the truck, and came back to close the garage door from the storm. Meredith got out of the car and shook his hand.

"Thanks for the tow. How much do I owe you?"

"Don't know. Haven't fixed your car yet."

She looked at him curiously. He pointed to the tow truck. For the first time, she noticed the sign on the side that read *Elmer's Wrecker Service.*

"I'm Elmer," he said with a grin.

"I would never have guessed," she said dryly. "Look, Elmer, I'm in a big hurry. I've got a plane to catch in Charleston in two hours. Do you think you can fix my car quickly?"

"Don't know if I can or not, lady. I got all these cars in front of ya." He waved his arm toward the parking area outside. Meredith turned and looked. There were no cars outside. There was no car in the service bay beside her. She looked back at Elmer who gave her another grin. They both laughed.

"I'll get right on it, but it might take a few minutes. If you want to wait, there's a diner next door. The food's not too good, but it's the only eatin' place in twenty miles. Besides, the coffee's OK."

"You don't own the diner, too, do you?"

"Nope. My wife, Emily, does."

Elmer rummaged behind the counter, found an umbrella, and escorted Meredith to the diner next door. A gray-haired woman greeted them as they entered.

"Howdy, Elmer. Who's your date?"

Meredith looked around. It was a simple diner with simple furniture — and a simple, fat-laden menu. The air was filled with the heavy smell of grease. In one booth sat the only customers, a couple looking tired and weary from eating. Their girth suggested that they had partaken of Emily's fried apples, sausage gravy, and biscuits on many occasions.

"This is . . ." Elmer stopped. "I don't believe I got your name."

"Meredith Grant. Professor Meredith Grant."

"Emily, this is Professor Meredith. She's got some car troubles, so while I'm a-fixin' it, why don't you fix her up a

25

hamburger and some fries."

"A small cup of coffee will do fine," suggested Meredith, looking uneasily at the menu posted on the wall.

"You sure?" asked Emily.

"Thanks, yes, coffee is fine. With all the excitement, I'm not hungry."

Actually, a hamburger hadn't passed through her lips in over ten years. The thought of one now made her nauseous.

"Well, professor," said Elmer, "you just sit tight and drink your coffee and settle down some. I'll do everything I can to help you catch your plane."

Elmer left the diner. Shortly after that, the hamburger-fries-sausage-and-gravy couple arose from their booth, paid their bill, and like two wandering rhinos, lumbered from the diner into the storm. Emily poured some coffee.

"Cream and sugar?"

"Black, please."

For Professor Grant, cream and sugar were taboo also. There was an uneasy silence as two clashing cultures attempted to find some common ground for small talk. After a considerable pause, Emily broke the silence.

"So you're tryin' to catch a plane?"

"Yes."

"Where ya goin'?"

"Chicago."

" Is that where ya live?"

"No. I live here in West Virginia. I teach at the University — Appalachian folklore."

"That's interestin'. Ever read the story of the ghost of Sleepy Holler?"

Meredith ignored the question and took a sip of coffee.

"I concentrate on establishing written confirmation of the oral traditions of the region. Consequently, I'm always rummaging in libraries — both private and public — flea markets — antique shops — estate auctions — looking for old books that may be of value to my research."

"That's nice." Emily could not have cared less. Her reading extended to TV Guide and an occasional National Inquirer. "Why ya goin' to Chicago?"

Meredith was a little put off by Emily's forwardness, but she was a captive of the situation and decided to make the most of it.

"To meet Donald, my fiancé," she replied.

"Your boyfriend, ya mean."

"Yes, my boyfriend," Meredith conceded with a blush. Somehow that description of the relationship embarrassed her. "He's a lawyer and travels quite a bit. Usually, we have to arrange meetings like this in order to see each other."

"Strange. You mean you fly all over the county just to see this guy?"

"Well, yes, I . . ." Meredith started to offer a more complete explanation, but decided it was pointless. She trailed off in mid-sentence, hiding her uneasiness in another sip of coffee.

"Sure, ya don't want a hamburger?"

Rain blew in as the door opened. It was three in the afternoon, but the sky was gray and dark — an ever engulfing darkness that only seemed to accentuate Meredith's feeling of isolation. Elmer shook the rain from his shoulders.

"Got some good news and some bad news for ya, lady. It's easy to fix — if I had the parts. And there's the problem. I ain't got the parts. Won't have until Monday. Got to ship it in from Charleston."

"There's no part store nearby?"

"Not that we can get to in this storm. Besides, they're not likely to have parts for a 1969 VW Beetle."

Emily was disappointed. Somehow she thought that a university professor, who flew around the country cavorting

27

with some three-piece lawyer dude, should be driving a BMW or Audi.

"Taxi?" asked Meredith.

"Are you kidding?"

"Bus?"

"Tuesdays and Thursdays. Besides, you're not going anywhere out there today. I hear on the radio the Gauley is risin' and will probably flood out the road between here and wherever you want to go before too long. Probably already has. If I were you, I'd head on down to the bed and breakfast for the night. Maybe in the morning we can get you back to Charleston."

"There's a bed and breakfast here?"

"Yep, right here on Loop Creek."

Meredith didn't quite believe him.

"Donald," she said, suddenly remembering her rendezvous, "what about Donald?"

"What about him?" asked Emily.

"He's headed for Chicago. You do have a phone, don't you?"

"Sure, but you have to crank it up," quipped Elmer.

Meredith looked at him incredulously. He grinned his broad-faced, apparently toothless grin.

"Don't pay any attention to him, honey," said Emily. "He jokes like that all the time. I got a push-button right here behind the counter."

Hurriedly, Meredith dialed a phone number, and without saying a word, hung-up.

"Beeper number," she explained.

A few minutes later the phone rang. It was Donald calling from the airport in Atlanta. In whispers, trying to gain some privacy, Meredith explained her hopeless situation. No, no, she was fine. No, no, there was no way to make the plane. They exchanged expressions of sorrow and

28

apologies. We'll meet next week. Where? Pittsburgh? Good. She could drive to Pittsburgh. Kisses and hugs. Miss you, too. Bye.

"Bed and breakfast, ma'am?" Elmer said as she hung up the phone.

"Bed and breakfast?" Meredith asked in return. "You mean there really is a bed and breakfast here? You weren't just kidding?"

"Best in the state, but it's a well-kept secret. They only serve the choosiest customers."

"I guess," she answered. She could visualize what this "bed and breakfast" was like. She shuttered and contemplated the possibility of sleeping in the car until her vivid, pessimistic imagination convinced her otherwise.

"Em'," said Elmer, "let's close up shop and take this young lady up to Billups' for the night."

Emily grabbed her keys and headed for the door. The three of them huddle together under Elmer's umbrella, braced themselves against the storm, and made their way to Emily's car.

"How long is this storm suppose to last?" Meredith asked as she settled into the back seat.

"Through the night," Elmer replied as they made their way down the narrow road.

The storm seemed to be intensifying as the rain poured over the windshield, and the wind buffeted the car from side to side. As they rounded a curve, the passenger compartment exploded with a flash of light that was accompanied by a loud thunderclap. For an instant, Meredith was blinded, but she could feel the car out of control. She could sense Elmer struggling with the steering wheel as the tires began to bounce wildly, indicating that the car had left the road. Elmer grunted. Emily expressed a small, passive "oh" (quite inappropriate for the occasion), and the car lurched to

29

a stop. Meredith was thrown forward, struck her head on the back of the front seat, and came rebounding to rest in the back seat. When all of the motion had ceased, she discovered herself sprawled across the seat, one foot resting against the window and the other dangling over the front seat. "Forgot your seat belt" was her first thought.

"Danged!" said Elmer. "You OK back there?"

Meredith slowly righted herself and did a quick self-examination. There was a small throbbing over her right eye, but other than the humiliation of being tossed around so unceremoniously, she was all right.

"I'm OK . . . What happened?"

"Must have got struck by lightning," said Elmer. "Let me see if I can get out of this ditch."

The storm had abruptly stopped.

Luckily, only the right tire was in the roadside ditch. With Emily at the wheel and a little muscle from Elmer, they were soon freed and back on the road. The storm began to rumble again, but there was only a slight drizzle of rain. The accident, coupled with the other events of the day, had drained Meredith both physically and emotionally. She looked out the left window at the shear cliffs as the car climbed the mountainside. She began to think of all of the dangerous possibilities should the storm return in full force. Her only desire now was for the safety of a house.

"Say, here's a place you might like to visit in the morning," said Emily.

They passed a small store on the left-hand side of the road. It was hanging precariously from the mountainside. The sign on the side of the store read:

The Book Binder
Rare and Unusual Books
An Opportunity of a Lifetime

Meredith leaned back in her seat and closed her eyes. The only opportunity she wanted now was a long, warm bath.

An hour later, Meredith found herself in a different world. She was now dressed in a borrowed calico dress. (She had inadvertently left her luggage at Elmer's station.) Refreshed by a bath in an antique, free-standing tub, she sat at a mahogany table, enjoying a classic country dinner with Mrs. Tillie, the innkeeper. The electricity was off because of the storm, but the room was filled with the glow of soft candlelight. Spread across the table were garden fresh beans, corn, squash, cucumbers, and other assorted delights. At first, she had considered refusing the chicken and dumplings, but Mrs. Tillie's warm, persuasive manner had won her over. Nobody can turn down Tillie Billups' dumplings she was told. Nobody. Not even Professor Meredith Grant. There was food for ten, but Meredith was the only house guest this evening. That impressed her as odd.

The house was immaculate and beautifully filled with rich wooden furniture — all antique — all well-made. The floors were made of well-polished oak with old-fashioned, high-board molding lining both the floor and the ceiling. The workmanship was unmatched. It was a perfect bed and breakfast. Tillie Billups should have been overbooked.

After dinner, they moved to the covered porch on the front of the house, overlooking the valley below. There were giants in the land that night as the storm had returned, thundering in all of its fury, but Meredith felt safe within the shelter of the porch. As lightning flashed, she and Mrs. Tillie would get a glimpse of the trees wrestling with the wind and the water tumbling from the mountainside, crossing the road, and rushing down toward the valley floor. Down there, somewhere, was her disabled car. Instinctively, she hoped a flash flood would not wash it away.

"So you're a university professor are you?" said Mrs. Tillie. She was an elderly lady who had obviously entertained many a guest in her day. She impressed Meredith as someone who had mastered the gentle art of hospitality and thoroughly enjoyed the exercise thereof. Through Tillie's gentle probing, Meredith found herself revealing everything important about her life — about her relationship with Donald — about her love for myths and legends — about her passion for rare books.

She told of her quest for the original diary of Aanosen Smith, a famous storyteller and researcher of mountain lore, who had lived during the Civil War. Many references to such a diary existed. Even excerpts were found in other books, but Aanosen's diary had never been found. However, the excerpts of his writings and the references to his diary were tantalizing, promising a gold mine of tales and legends, if found. Some even claimed that many of the legends were true, and Aanosen's diary contained the proof and the key to new and mystical worlds. That is why Meredith combed the estate sales and flea markets of Appalachia. That is what had brought her by chance to Billups' Bed and Breakfast on this stormy night.

As Meredith talked and Mrs. Tillie listened, the evening quickly grew late. But the storm continued. Finally, Mrs. Tillie gathered her shawl around her shoulders.

"Come with me, child. I have something interesting to show you."

The two women rose together, and Mrs. Tillie led them into the house. The electricity was still out, and the house was lit by candlelight, creating a distinctively primitive, yet comforting, atmosphere. They arrived at the library and stopped at the entrance. Mrs. Tillie proceeded into the room and lit a couple of large candles. As she turned toward Meredith, the candlelight glistened in her eyes.

"Be my guest, child," she said. "Explore."

Meredith began to examine the books, and as she did, her wonderment grew. Every book in the library was over a hundred years old. Many of them were relatively rare. Although she had seen a number of these books in other libraries, she had never before seen so many books of this type in one place, in one collection. The possibilities were enormous. Perhaps Mrs. Tillie Billups had other rare books in her collection. Perhaps she had the original works of Aanosen Smith. Meredith was almost afraid to ask the question.

"Mrs. Tillie, would you happen to have the —"

"The diary of Aanosen Smith? No, child, I don't. But I know someone who may."

"Who is that?"

"The Book Binder — Obadiah Jones."

Immediately, Meredith remembered the little store clinging to the hillside. Immediately, she recalled what the sign had said — *Rare and Unusual Books* — *An Opportunity of a Lifetime.* This was too good to be true. She would not allow her hopes to be raised. She had been close before. At least, she had believed that she had been close before, only to have her spirits dashed in disappointment. In truth, she believed that she never would find that diary. In truth, she believed there was a good possibility that, like any myth or legend, Aanosen's diary didn't exist at all. Nevertheless, thoughts began to swirl simultaneously through her head: the whole chain of events that had led her to this house — the reality of this incredible library hidden upon a remote mountainside — the impossibility of a rare bookstore that she had never heard of. There was suddenly life, vitality, and possibility in her quest.

"Yes, the Book Binder," she said as nonchalantly as she could, "I remember seeing the store on the way up here."

33

"I have never asked him for a book that he could not find," announced Tillie. "I'm sure he can find your Aanosen Smith for you."

"Yes, perhaps. I must visit him in the morning."

Obadiah. Obadiah Jones, thought Meredith. Who was Obadiah Jones? She had met with many rare-book dealers. She had been to conferences and symposiums. She had corresponded often with the well-connected. But she had never heard of Obadiah Jones. She couldn't wait for morning to come.

Indeed, the following morning found Meredith standing outside The Book Binder. She had risen early and dined on fresh fruit and toast with Mrs. Tillie. The storm had passed, being replaced with a cool, bright morning. The crisp rain-washed air stood in stark contrast to the maelstrom from the night before. According to Mrs. Tillie, the distance from the inn to Elmer's was only a couple of miles. Consequently, Meredith had decided on a country-morning hike, a hike that would lead her directly passed Obadiah Jones' store. So there she stood, hesitating at the door. For some strange reason, she felt so foolish about the whole adventure. After all, why would anyone believe that anything of value could be found here at this rickety looking store? The sides were covered with tar paper. The window sills were bent and crooked. Even the tin roof showed signs of coming loose and falling to the valley below. For a brief moment, Meredith almost turned to walk away, but her curiosity finally ruled. Slowly, she pushed open the door and walked inside.

The inside was filled with a heavy, musty, familiar smell. It was the type of smell that always overcomes a building that has been abandoned or neglected — a smell that cannot be removed with any amount of perfumes, air-fresheners, or cleaning. She had encounter this smell before as a child while rummaging through the old abandoned

34

"company" store in the coal town where she grew up. She had found this odor in the cedar chest at her great-grandmother's house shortly before she died. And she had, on more than one occasion, associated this vile smell with old libraries — graveyards actually — where books, once alive and vibrant with their authors' words, were left to die and rot away in obscurity. To her, it was a melancholy smell of lost dreams.

"May I help you, child?" a shaky voice asked from the doorway that led to the back of the store.

A small, humped-shouldered man stood in the shadows of the room. There were no lights, and the store was lit only by the sun streaming through a solitary window on one side of the room. The man shuffled forward, assisted by a cane. As he emerged from the shadows, Meredith could see that he indeed was very small, considerably less than five feet tall. He sported a short, scruffy, red beard, and his hair sprayed out from his head like sagebrush. He repeated the question.

"The name's Obadiah Jones. May I help you, child?"

His deep green eyes sparkled.

"Yes, yes," she said lamely, "I'm looking for a book."

"Then you've come to the right place, child. You've come to the right place, indeed."

He spread his arms wide open, and looking around the room, gazed deliberately into each corner. And as he did, Meredith, for the first time, realized that the store was filled with books. There were shelves along each wall, reaching to the ceiling. Boxes of books were scattered around the bare hardwood floor. She could see through the door to the storage area in the back where even more boxes were piled in apparent disarray.

But what caught her eye were two bookcases mounted with glass doors. The doors were closed and locked by

35

small golden padlocks. One case stood upright behind the counter at the back wall, and one case, in the form of a table, was positioned in front of the counter. It was positioned in a manner that allowed one to look down through the glass to see its contents.

"I think you'd be interested in seeing these," said Obadiah, gently taking her hand.

He led her to the counter where she could better see the locked, upright bookcase. In the dim light, she could see numerous books, written in almost every language and tongue. Each one was wrapped with a golden ribbon. She readily recognized Latin and Greek, but there were others that she could only guess. Was that Egyptian or Mayan hieroglyphics? Was that Hebrew?

"You see this book?" Obadiah asked, pointing to a volume written in Greek.

"Yes," said Meredith, "what is it?"

"It's the original Chronicles of Alexander the Great written by Aristarcus."

Impossible, thought Meredith, that's impossible. The Chronicles of Alexander were lost when his library was destroyed by fire in 300 AD. There was no way this old hillbilly could have acquired that book. No way. It was obviously a fake. And Obadiah Jones, The Book Binder, was a fraud. Meredith heard her voice whisper her initial thought: "Impossible."

"Oh, no. Not at all, young lady. Not at all. Not when you have the right connections." He paused to redirect her attention to the bookcase. Slowly, he read the titles, "The Mayan Book of The Dead, The Satire of Menippus, The Chronicles of Ramasees — "

"Fake. They're all fake. These cannot possibly be authentic."

"Oh, indeed? What makes you so sure?"

Meredith conceived a test. "How much to you want for them? No, no, this one. How much to you want for this one?" She pointed to an Egyptian scroll.

"They're not for sale. You see, they have already been bound."

"They've what?"

"They've already been bound, and I can only bind a book once, you know." He paused. "Or perhaps you don't."

What on earth did he mean, she asked herself. By now, Meredith was convinced that the man was a fraud and definitely on the strange side. He might impress some unsuspecting tourist with his fake books and strange talk about binding, but she was ready to leave.

"I must be going," she said and turned to walk away.

"But wait. You haven't inspected the other bookcase. I think you will find what you are looking for there."

The words were spoken with such reassuring authority that they stopped her against her will.

"And what would that be?" she asked.

"The diary of Aanosen Smith, of course. That is what you've been looking for, isn't it? A relatively easy book to come by, I might say."

At first, the words took Meredith by surprise, and her heart raced into her throat. How did he know that? How could he know that? Perhaps his claims were true. Perhaps — no — Mrs. Tillie, of course. Somehow he had spoken to Mrs. Tillie, and she had told him about her quest for Aanosen Smith's diary.

"Do you want to see it?"

"Of course," she heard herself say. She began to scold herself. Why are you going along with this man, this charlatan? Why are you allowing him to lead you on? Meredith Grant, why don't you just turn and walk out that door right now? Right now! Go on. This man has nothing for you but

37

seducing words and lies.

"It's right here, child. Come and see for yourself."

As if in a trance, she found herself moving to the table. It was as if someone else was in her body, and she was only a passive observer. She could sense her eyes looking down at the dozen or so books that lay under glass on the table. Her attention was drawn to a book whose title, in hand-written letters, read: *The Diary of Aanosen Smith, Life Beyond the Myths.* She had seen that handwriting before in some of Aanosen's letters that had survived. It looked authentic.

"May I inspect it?" she heard herself say.

"But, of course, child." Obadiah reached into his pocket, extracted a small key, unlocked the glass case, and lifted the book gently from its resting place. "But I must ask that you touch it with only one hand."

A strange request, but she obediently complied and began browsing through the pages with her left hand behind her back. If this was a forgery, it was a very good forgery. The handwriting was Aanosen's all right, but why would anyone want to forge the diary of Aanosen Smith? Only a handful of people knew who he was, and, although his diary might be a great academic find, its monetary value was nominal.

"How much do you want for it?" she heard herself ask.

"It's not for sale. None of the books in this case are for sale." He leaned closer and whispered, "But I can bind it for you."

There was that nonsensical talk again about binding the book. She drew back from the book, realizing that he was only enticing her to eventually pay more. Yes, that was what he was doing — baiting her by pretending to be unwilling to sell it. He placed the book back on the table, and Meredith took a step backward.

"I must be going," she said clumsily as she continued to back toward the door. "I must go see about my car."

Within seconds, she found herself outside, walking briskly down the road toward Elmer's garage. As she was walking, she attempted to analyze the situation. Was the book real or fake? What was Obadiah Jones up to? If it was real — and she was beginning to believe against logic that it was — would he eventually sell it to her for a reasonable price? After all, she had only so much grant money for her project.

The news at Elmer's was not encouraging. It would be afternoon before the part would arrive, but he assured her that she would be safely home before bedtime. Meredith went next door to the diner and paged Donald. During a lengthy call, she related to him the events since they had last spoken. She described Tillie Billups and her marvelous inn. They must return there together someday. She also recounted her encounter with Obadiah Jones, the Book Binder, and spoke of the very real possibility that she had actually found the book of her quest. Donald was pleased indeed. They would celebrate her triumph should she persuade the old man to sell the book to her. And, oh, by the way, he could advance her any funds needed for the transaction. No limit.

Meredith left Elmer's with a renewed purpose. While telling her story to Donald, she had convinced herself that the book was real. The reality of that conviction overwhelmed her with excitement. With a little hard-nosed negotiating, she would soon have her prized possession. She was not going to let old Obadiah control the situation the way he had before. She was not going to let him smooth-talk or psycho-babble his way to her disadvantage. No. She was going to march right into his store and make him a straight-out offer. No deals. No haggling. No wavering. No game playing. And that's exactly what she did.

"Mr. Jones," she said, standing in the middle of the store, "I want to buy that book. I'll give you $1,000 for it."

Obadiah was behind the counter, rummaging through a box of books. He barely looked up.

"It's not for sale."

"$1,500."

"I told you, child, it's not for sale."

Meredith bit her lip. "All right then, $2,000."

"Child, I cannot sell you this book, but I can bind it for you."

Meredith was becoming frustrated by the man's refusal to deal and flustered by his nonsensical talk about binding the book.

"Mr. Jones, name your price. Any price."

"A book like this is priceless, child. You cannot buy it. The only way you can possess it is for me to bind it for you. That's what I've been trying to tell you all along. The book cannot be bought. It must be bound, and the binding, of course, is absolutely free."

"So you can bind it for me?" she asked.

"Yes, yes," said Obadiah, his green eyes sparkling.

"And then it will be mine?"

Obadiah nodded his head. "And then, my child, you will possess it."

Meredith drew in a deep breath. "OK, Mr. Jones. Bind the book for me."

"Are you sure?"

She was growing tired of his games. First he wanted to bind the book. Now he's not so sure.

"Yes, yes," she said impatiently, "go on, bind the book for me."

The old man came from behind the counter and unlocked the case. Carefully, he removed the book with one

40

hand and held it before him. Turning toward her, he motioned firmly for her to come closer.

"I'll need your help," he said.

She approached the table and stood facing the old man.

"Hold out your hands," he commanded, "and relax."

Meredith had no idea what was going to happen, but she was committed to play along as long as, in the end, she could walk out of that store with Aanosen's diary. She held out her hands, and Obadiah placed the book gently into them.

"Now open it," he said.

Meredith looked down at him. She looked full and long into his deep green eyes.

"I said open it, child."

Meredith obeyed. The book now lay open in her outstretched hands. At first, she felt nothing, but gradually a warm glow began to radiate from the book into her hands. The warmth traveled up her forearms and passed her elbows. It was a strange, reassuring glow that invited more and more of her body to participate. She soon discovered that she could not let go of the book as the warmth now extended to her shoulders.

"What is this?" she said, bewildered, yet excited by the warmth that was overtaking her. Her whole body was now engulfed in a warmth that was beginning to increase in intensity and pulsate from the pages of the book.

"The binding has begun, child. The binding has begun."

The pulsating warmth increased even more and Meredith soon sensed nothing else. Obadiah and his store passed from her consciousness as the warmth grew and grew until blackness overtook her.

Meredith was gone, and Obadiah Jones stood alone in the middle of the store. Carefully, deliberately, he picked up a book that was lying in the floor. Wrapping it with a

41

golden ribbon, he placed it in the bookcase behind the counter. And locking the golden padlock, he returned to rummaging through a pile of his books. The binding had been completed.

Two days later, Donald accompanied a State Police Officer as they knocked on the door of Billups Bed and Breakfast. A young woman opened the door.

"Morning, ma'am. I'm Sergeant Drake, State Police. May we ask you some questions?"

"Yes, yes," she said, a little unnerved by his presence.

"Do you have a guest by the name of Meredith Grant?"

"Professor," interjected Donald.

"Professor Meredith Grant," echoed Drake.

"No. I don't believe I do," she said slowly.

"Was she here this past weekend?"

"No, sir. No one by that name has been here."

"Tillie Billups, the inn keeper. Is she here?"

"What?" said the young woman, clearly surprised by the question.

"I said is Tillie Billups here? I'd like to question her."

The young woman stared at him in disbelief.

"Sir, where did you get that name?"

"From Meredith Grant," said Donald. "She phoned me two days ago and told me she was staying at Tillie Billups' Bed and Breakfast."

"And she told you she talked with Tillie?"

"Yes."

"Then," said the young lady with a sigh, "I suggest you check out the family graveyard on the hill over there. You see, Tillie Billups was my great-great grandmother who lived during the Civil War. She founded this bed and breakfast over a hundred years ago. But she died in 1882. So if your Meredith Grant, whoever she is, has been talking to Tillie Billups, then she's probably up there at the family graveyard, too ."

* * * * * *

The deep shadows of the woods were slowly giving way to the morning sun as Meredith sat upon the porch swing. A cool breeze barely kissed her neck and brought with it the smell of honeysuckle. Perhaps today would be a good day to pick some berries for cobbler pie. A rush of wind raced across the ridges, causing the heavy dew from the night before to spray down around the porch on which she sat. The only sounds were those of anonymous animals, rising from their sleep to change place with their nocturnal cousins. Meredith was at peace with the morning. The quiet creaking of a screen door signaled the approach of Mrs. Tillie with a breakfast snack. Meredith didn't even bother to turn, but continued to watch the day unfold in the valley below.

"Morning, Mrs. Tillie."

"Morning, child. Care for some coffee and sweet rolls?"

"Yes, thanks. I believe I do."

Mrs. Tillie set the tray down and took up her position in the rocker.

"Ummm. These are delicious," said Meredith. "Just how did you manage to learn to cook like this, Mrs. Tillie?"

"Practice, child. And plenty of time for trial and error."

They sat quietly for a long time, nibbling on the rolls and sipping the strong, black coffee. There was no hurry this morning. That was the whole point of the morning — to deliberately take it in slowly. As they gazed out over the trees, a small movement far below on the path leading up the mountain caught Tillie's eye. She stood up to investigate further. The movement became larger and larger until she could clearly see a man dressed in a Union uniform,

43

riding a chestnut mare. He sat tall in the saddle, his hat accentuating his height.

"He's on his way," whispered Tillie with excitement.

Meredith rose to join her at the banister.

"I told you he'd be here sooner or later," said Tillie, smiling triumphantly.

"Aanosen?" asked Meredith.

"Who else, child, would you be looking for?"

For an instant, she thought of Donald. But it was only for an instant. After all, the mythical man of her dreams was about to arrive.

♠ ♠ ♠ ♠ ♠ ♠ ♠ ♠ ♠ ♠ ♠ ♠

Ordinary Heroes

♠ ♠ ♠ ♠ ♠ ♠ ♠ ♠ ♠ ♠ ♠ ♠

I am forty-seven years old, and I've never seen my father cry. We've been to funerals and weddings, sickbeds and births, but through all those years, I have never seen him cry. It is truly ironic how you can know someone for so many years and still they have secrets to tell.

We were visiting recently with my folks. They had forsaken Loop Creek and the hills of West Virginia years ago to live in the Piedmont area near Winston-Salem, North Carolina — Tobaccoville to be exact. In fact, they now live in the shadow of Pilot Mountain and Mt. Airy, just down the road from Aunt Bea's kitchen. Places made famous by Andy Griffith, Barney Fife, and crew.

Mom and Dad had just returned from Baltimore where they had attended a reunion for World War II merchant marines. There is a place in Baltimore harbor that reunites these crusty old sailors, giving them an opportunity to retell their stories and relive the "glory days" of the war. In the afternoon, an old boat takes them and their spouses for a cruise in the bay where they can try their hand again at sailing, encounter a surprise enemy air attack, and pay tribute to those who had died in battle. Although the merchant marines were not part of the military, they were, nonetheless, deeply involved in the war. When your ship is carrying supplies to the front lines, you are just as much a target as a battle cruiser or an aircraft carrier.

On the day of our visit, Dad was as talkative as you will

45

ever find him. He is usually a quiet person who talks only about his gardening, or woodworking, or mechanical inventions. But on that day he was full of memories. Oh, I had heard some of the stories before — about how he had run off at fifteen-and-a-half to Norfolk and signed up on a ship headed straight into the European theater of war. However, this time there were some new revelations.

"Johnny, everybody was surprised that I had kept all my records. Everybody else was straining, trying to remember what ship they were on and when. But I had it all there in my little folder."

"You mean you have all your records?"

"Yep, let me show you."

He got up from the kitchen table and went into the bedroom. A minute later he came back with a small folder — the kind you use might use to store insurance policies. He laid it on the table and pulled out a handful of certificates, handing them to me. I began to read — the *L. L. Lillington*, the *Victory Star*. The list went on with each ship and the date of service.

"Yep, everybody was surprised that I had kept all this stuff. Everybody else had lost theirs. And look at these."

He handed me a stack of smaller certificates. They were citations of service.

I began to read again, "The European War Zone, The Mediterranean War Zone, The Pacific War Zone. Now wait a minute, Dad. When were you in the Pacific?"

"What's this?" he said, handing me a picture.

"The Suez Canal?"

"Try again."

"The Panama?"

"Right. And what's on the other side of the Panama?"

"The Pacific."

"Right. Spent a year and a half in the Pacific."

46

Dad had spent a year and half of his life in the Pacific, and I was just then finding out about it.

"We came back around the tip of South America. Spent time in Brazil and Port-a-Prince before being discharged in Galveston, Texas. See this picture? That's me and Houston — the best buddy I ever had. We went everywhere together. Just a couple of kids in the middle of a war. He got swept overboard in the North Atlantic." Dad said it so matter-of-factly that it seemed like a natural, everyday occurrence. "I remember me and Houston there in Galveston. We ran out of money and were out of work. We were hungry, real hungry, so we joined the circus."

"What?! You're kidding."

"No, really. Barnum and Bailey Circus. We got a job putting up tents. We worked for 'em for five days. Got paid five dollars. But when we finally got to Baton Rouge, we quit. The work was too hard. (They had been on ships in the middle of a combat zone, and the circus work was too hard!?) So there was me and Houston. No money. Hungry. No ship. So we got to watching the milkman in the morning. He'd go from house to house, picking up money out of the empty bottles and leaving fresh milk on the door steps. Well, we started going in front of him and pickin' up the money and behind him and drinkin' the milk. We lived pretty good for a couple of weeks until we managed to catch us another ship headed for Europe."

Dad and I continued on for a while as he showed me more pictures and certificates, and I marveled that all of this had been preserved. Dad came upon another picture.

"That's me and Houston again."

There were three other young men in the picture, but he couldn't remember their names, only Houston's.

"We were in Antwerp harbor during the Battle Of the Bulge. We were sort of trapped there in the harbor and

47

didn't have a whole lot to do except watch the bombs drop. One night, we were sittin' on the dock, watchin' the buzz-bombs come into the city when someone suggested we go up on deck to get a better view. We had no sooner boarded ship and looked back when — wham! — a bomb hit right on the dock where we had been standing. You were always close to dying, but never really thought about it much. At least, you tried not to."

He paused to look at another old, tattered picture.

"You know there were times when the sea was as smooth as glass, and you could look out and see a hundred — a hundred and fifty ships — sitting on the horizon like a bunch of toys. And then there were other times, when the sea was so rough and angry you couldn't see any of those ships around you. From time to time, you would see one rise up on a wave in the distance and quickly sink back down into the sea. And then you'd rise up on the crest of a wave and see a ship or two off on the horizon. But the other ships were buried from sight beneath the waves.

"I remember one time when we were in 'hot' water — enemy subs were in the area. I was stationed out on the bow as a lookout. The sea was extremely rough that day, and the waves were sweeping over the bow. Well, after a while, they called me and told me all was clear, and I could come back inside. But when I turned and looked at the waves rushing across that deck, I knew I couldn't make it. I was stuck out on that bow in the middle of the North Atlantic. And it was freezin' cold. It so happened that there was a little storage area about half the size of a refrigerator out there on the bow. So I crawled back up in there as best I could for protection. For months, the heels of my feet were numb from being in that little box. I spent that night, curled up in that little cubbyhole, rollin' and reelin' with the waves, crying and scared to death — certain I was gonna

48

get swept overboard like Houston."

He put down the picture that he was holding and smiled at me.

"I met a man there in Baltimore last week. We had been in the same section, but never could figure out if we had sailed on the same ship together. He said he had enlisted when he was fifteen. I told him I had, too. I asked him what he did during the war. He said mostly he was scared and homesick and cried a lot. Especially at night."

Dad paused again and smiled a wistful smile.

"I told him, yeah, me too."

True heroes: Ordinary people in extraordinary circumstances.

The River Runs Cold in February

The river runs cold in February
Where potbellied men beside a potbellied stove,
With conversations crude and bold
And half truths spread with sincere smiling,
Weave their tales of conquest.
The wind blows cold in February
Where balding men wrestle balding tires
Amidst talk of tools and motors old
As fingers cold and half-warmed aching
Arch impatiently over embers bright.
The snow falls cold in February
Where aging men resuscitate aging cars,
Breathing fumes of gas and miracle oils
As withered leaves, the dregs of summer,
Blow aimlessly before the mountain storms.
They speak not at all of friendship,
Yet confirm it
With every tale of deer and bow and hunting knife —
Or predictions of spring or snow.
And all the while, amidst considerable joke and jest,
They dream of dancing — dancing — dancing.
Of young summer dancing.
In the moonlight warm dancing.
With the buxom lass dancing.
Through the springtime of their lives.

♠ ♠ ♠ ♠ ♠ ♠ ♠ ♠ ♠ ♠ ♠ ♠ ♠ ♠ ♠ ♠ ♠ ♠

To Bean or Not to Bean
(That is the Question!)
1961

By Little Johnny

♠ ♠ ♠ ♠ ♠ ♠ ♠ ♠ ♠ ♠ ♠ ♠ ♠ ♠ ♠ ♠ ♠ ♠

You never know what's gonna come crawlin' out of these mountains. That's why me and Bucky like fishin', especially along Loop Creek. Now, it's just a small, rocky stream that has a lot of trouble holdin' water in the summer time. But it's got a lot of sink holes that go deep into the earth. Bucky and me just know that these sink holes connect up to some vast underground ocean — or at least to the lake across the mountain — where giant bass and blue gill swim free. And we just know that someday we're gonna land the big one. Of course, neither one of us likes to eat fish. So we'll probably just get it mounted and hang it on our wall. That way, someday, we can show our grandkids the giant sea bass that we caught in Loop Creek. A fella can dream, can't he?

But if you really want to know the real reason we like fishin' in Loop Creek, it's because there ain't nothin' else. The nearest river is fifteen miles away, and when you're thirteen and your basic mode of transportation is a bike, it might as well be a hundred. So for psychological as well as practical purposes, Loop Creek is the only place to fish.

Anyway, me and Bucky were down by Scrapper's Sink Hole seinin' for minnows when we caught this thing that turned our whole lives around. When we pulled up our net, instead of a bunch of minnows, this thing was just lyin' there all wet and red and slimy like a hunk of beef liver. Honest. At first, Bucky thought it was deer innards or something like that. So we drug it up on the bank and laid it on a rock to get a better look.

"It's deer guts," proclaimed Bucky.

"Well, if it is, it's still alive. Look, it's breathin' or quiverin' or somethin'," I said.

Bucky took off his hat and bent down for a closer look. His nose was practically touchin' the thing when suddenly he jerked back, startled. For an instant, my attention was on Bucky, and when I looked back at our deer guts, it had miraculously sprouted a head and legs and was desperately attemptin' to escape. Fortunately, one of its new-found legs was tangled up in the net.

"Quick! Get the bucket!" yelled Bucky.

As I ran for the bucket, Bucky took the net and wrapped it around the creature. We dumped the whole thing in the bucket, and when we did, our creature turned back into deer guts. It was one of the craziest, scariest things I'd ever seen. From that day forward, it made me more than a little leery of Scrapper's Sink Hole.

"What is that thing?" I asked.

"Beats me," said Bucky. "Let's take it up to the fillin' station and see if Eddie knows."

So we beat a path for the fillin' station. It was the local hangout where all the men (and boys) along the creek exchanged gossip and competed in lyin' contests. You know — who shot the biggest deer, who's got the fastest car, who's datin' the prettiest girl — things like that. When we arrived, the usual crew was sittin' on the three-foot wall beside the station.

First off, there was Eddie Brown, the bear of a gas station attendant, sweatin' like he'd actually done some work. Eddie was a kind ol' soul whose main ambition in life was to pump gas and fix tires. But he was good at what he did. He was especially proud of his collection of assorted nails, screws, and other things that he had pulled from flat tires. He kept them in a case that hung prominently on the wall at the station. Kinda like a butterfly collection. Eddie was always chewin' tobacco, and he always had a stain or two on his shirt. But anyone who'd give you six pieces of gum for a nickel (instead of five) was OK in my book. And, of course, if there was any goings-on on the creek, Eddie knew all about it.

And then there was Hodgekins, the local loiterer and philosopher. Hodgekins didn't have a first name or maybe he didn't have a last name — he was simply Hodgekins. He was at the fillin' station as much as Eddie, except he didn't get paid for bein' there. I suppose he just wanted to be where the action was. Of course, as local philosopher, he was always givin' his slant on why things were the way they were, why they weren't the way they oughta be, why they weren't the way they seemed, or why they seemed the way they weren't — or something like that. Just name the topic, and Hodgekins would talk your ears off.

The final member of the fillin' station crew was Grit McCormick, the resident huntin' champion. Grumpy old Grit knew everything there was to know about huntin' and trappin' in these mountains. He'd seen everything in these woods: red-spotted bears, gray panthers, albino rattlesnakes. He'd even claimed to have seen alligators and a Big Foot. That's where he lost me. Everybody knows alligators don't live this far north.

Anyway, Eddie, Hodgekins, and Grit were at their usual stations on the wall, kickin' the back out-a their shoes, wavin' at the cars goin' by, and killin' the grass behind them with tobacco juice. We came runnin' up and showed the contents of our bucket to the experts.

"Deer guts," said Eddie.

"No, no," said Grit. "If this is what I think it is, it's the most dangerous animal alive." He looked up from the bucket, and squintin' his eyes, peered at everybody who had crowded around. "Very rare. Very rare, indeed. I remember Grandpa Napoleon tellin' about one of these years ago. It just came slimin' into town one day and took up residence in the church well. The death and destruction was terrible."

Everybody looked at Grit with blank stares. None of us had a clue to what he was talkin' about.

"Napoleon lost half his coon dogs, and Jesse Smith lost three newborn heifers."

"Grit," interrupted Eddie Brown, "just what in the world are you talkin' about?"

"It's a devil catfish, Eddie," said Grit. "A devil catfish from the depths of hell."

"It's deer guts," insisted Hodgekins.

"No," said Bucky. "It moves. It changes shape. It nearly bit my nose off."

"See," said Grit. "Told ya so."

"Let's get a better look at this thing," said Eddie Brown. He led us behind the station to an old chest-type Coca Cola cooler. "Here, empty it into this."

Bucky lifted the bucket and dumped the contents into the cooler, net and all. Almost immediately the thing sprung a head, a tail, and legs and began to fight against the net which had it trapped. It looked a little like a giant blood-red salamander with black spots around its head, but it had teeth like a fox or raccoon and claws like a bear. Its tail was long and snake-like. Hodgekins claimed he saw rattlers on the end of it.

"Man, oh, man," exclaimed Eddie, takin' off his hat and

54

wipin' his brow. "Ain't never seen anything like that. Where'd ya catch it?"

"Scrapper's Sink Hole," I said.

"Yep," announced Grit, "it's a devil catfish all right. We'd better kill it before it kills all the dogs on the creek. Or worse yet, some small child."

"Now, wait a minute, Grit," said Eddie. "It ain't goin' nowhere but this cooler. And ya ain't gonna kill it, either. I bet the game warden would be real interested in seein' this thing. Might even get these boys' picture in the paper."

"Ya better kill it," insisted Grit, "before it's too late."

"Look!" said Hodgekins. "It's done turned back into deer guts."

Sure enough, the creature had turned back into deer guts. The best we could tell was that somehow it curled itself up into a ball so you couldn't see its head and legs. Someone suggested we try to get the net loose so it wouldn't hurt itself when it decided to pop back out. That's when Bucky made his fateful mistake.

"Let me try," he said.

He reached into the cooler and was in the middle of untanglin' the net when the creature sprung back to life.

"Yipes!" cried Bucky, pullin' back a bloody hand. "It bit me!"

As Grit slammed the cooler door shut, Bucky danced around the yard, shakin' his hand and moanin' something fierce. The long and the short of it was that his hand swelled up like a snakebite, and he ran a fever for three or four days. At first, he told his Mom that he had been snake bit, so she called Doc Dailey, who came over and gave him a snakebite shot. That only made his behind swell up and itch like a bad case of poison ivy. I'm tellin' ya, he was in real miserable shape for several days, passin' in and out of consciousness, and mumblin' strange things about old

55

Scapper's Sink Hole.

I went to the fillin' station the next day after the bitin' episode to check on ol' Be-elzebub. That's the name I gave to the devil catfish. I had to consult my Bible to come up with that one. It made me right proud. When I got to the station, I found ol' Hodgekins and Grit standin' over the counter, goin' nose to nose in a heated debate. The only thing that separated them was a five-gallon jar of pickled pigs feet.

It's strange how your mind wanders. That jar of pickled pigs feet had been sittin' on that counter for as long as I could remember — right next to the jar of giant dill pickles and the purple pickled eggs. But I don't ever recall anyone eatin' any. I mean, have you ever heard someone say, "I got this real hankerin' to run down to the fillin' station and get a Coca-Cola and a mess of pickled pigs feet?" I haven't. Even Grit wouldn't touch the things. Now I ask you, who in their right mind would ever come up with the idea of pickled pigs feet in the first place? It must have been a monumental freak accident of nature that led to *that* recipe. Come to think of it, when it comes to weirdness, purple pickled eggs ain't far behind.

Pickled pigs feet aside, there was Grit and Hodgekins in heated discussion, goin' nose to nose.

"Grit, ya ain't gonna kill that varmint. We're gonna keep it for scientific investigation."

"I am gonna kill it, Hodgekins — as a community service."

"Let me ask you somethin', Grit. What did you do with that albino rattlesnake?"

"I killed it, of course."

"And the spotted red bear?"

"Same thing. Shot it plum-dead right through the left temple."

56

"And what about Earl Craddock?"

"Now wait a minute, Hodgekins, that ain't fair. I just winged him in the shoulder."

"But you thought he was a silver ringed-tail squirrel, didn't ya?"

"That ain't the point, Hodgekins," protested Grit, his face turnin' red and the veins on his neck bulgin' out. "This thing is dangerous."

"So you're gonna kill it. Is that your answer to everything? Don't you know that a man ought to be killin' things for only one reason — to eat and to live. Grit, you can't go around killin' everything that moves just because it moves. That's upsettin' the natural order of things."

"I'll tell ya what's upsettin' the natural order of things. It's your science with all of its radioactive A-bombs. That's what probably spawned this here devil catfish."

Nope, I thought, pickled pigs feet is what I'd call upsettin' the natural order of things. Why, they're probably just as lethal as ol' Be-elzebub.

Grit and Hodgekins stayed at each other for some time, arguin' back and forth. But Eddie stayed out of the whole fracas, quietly sittin' in the corner chewin' his tobacco. Eventually, Grit got tired of reason, headed out to his truck, and despite Hodgekins' protests, pulled out his shotgun. The four of us marched around back to the old Coca-Cola cooler.

"Open the cooler, Eddie," command Grit, raisin' his gun to his shoulder.

"Ya can't do this, Grit," pleaded Hodgekins.

"Watch me," spat Grit. "Now stand back, Eddie, and open 'er up."

Eddie slowly opened the lid, and Grit crept closer and closer, his gun raised, until he could see inside. To our surprise, it was empty.

"I let it loose early this mornin'," said Eddie. "You both are wrong. It's a wild animal, a child-a-nature. It doesn't deserve to be killed, and it doesn't deserve to be locked up — even for scientific investigation."

Grit dropped his gun, and Hodgekins slapped his thigh with his cap in disgust. Ol' Be-elzebub had left a green slime streak down one side of the cooler that eventually ate the "a" off the word "Cola." We followed its slime trail across the road and down to the creek where it disappeared into the water. Ol' Be-elzebub had, indeed, escaped. Along with it, five of the best bird dogs in the area soon disappeared, too. Grit claimed the devil catfish was to blame. Survival of the meanest and orneriest — now that's what I'd call the natural order of things, wouldn't you?

A month later, me and Bucky were sittin' on his back porch, tryin' to figure out what to do with the day. The preacher had been preachin' lately about how we ought to make the most of each day. He'd say things like: "This is the first day of the rest of your life." and "Make the most of every moment." and "Seize every opportunity to live life to its fullest." and things like that. I'd been wonderin' about that lately. Just how were you supposed to make the most of the day with a head cold and stomach cramps? And what about when your teacher piles tons of homework on ya? How are you supposed to enjoy the day when that happens? Anyway, the preacher had made me feel kinda guilty lately for not usin' every single moment in some kinda productive activity. I wondered what he would say about the half hour me and Bucky had just wasted throwin' rocks at the chipmunks?

It was now autumn, and the leaves were just about at their peak, and like I said, we were tryin' to figure out how to "seize the moment." As we sat there, Bucky began rubbin' the back of his hand where the devil catfish had bitten him, and he got this far-off, misty-eyed look on his face. Then he just stood up and looked off into the woods like he was some kinda zombie.

"We're gonna eat quail tomorrow," he announced. "Let's go squirrel huntin'."

"Sounds like a good idea to me," I said, even though I wasn't too sure what his quail announcement had to do with goin' squirrel huntin'.

We got our shotguns and began to climb the mountain in back of his house. There was a stand of hickory back at the head of the hollow that was legendary for squirrel huntin'. At least that's what Bucky claimed, but me and him had hunted back there several times and never once saw a squirrel. Still yet, Bucky claimed that that stand of hickory was a squirrel mecca — whatever mecca meant.

Have you ever hunted quail? What happens is that old bird hides in a thicket until the last minute. Then when you're right on top of him, he takes off in a loud rush, his wings flappin' something fierce with leaves a-flyin' all over the place. Now, if you're huntin' quail, ya kinda expect one to fly up in your face at any moment. But when you're huntin' squirrel and one of those quails comes thunderin' up out of the bushes, your heart can just drop right down into your stomach. And that's exactly what happened to me and Bucky. I was followin' him along the trail as we neared the hickory stand when the bushes exploded in front of us. I thought ol' Be-elzebub had returned to take its revenge. As the bird flew off, Bucky raised his gun and winged it enough so that it couldn't fly.

"Shoot!" he shouted.

But I couldn't. He was in my line of sight, and my hands were still shakin' from surprise. Frightened, the quail ran in front of us to the right. Bucky shot again. Then the old bird switched and ran back toward the left, where I finally got off a shot and missed. And then it came runnin' right at us. (I've never heard of anyone bein' gored by a quail, but I guess there's always a first time.) The old bird shot right passed Bucky and darted through my legs. Bucky whirled and aimed his gun, which was pointing directly at my midsection.

"Duck!" he shouted.

Instinctively, I turned my back to Bucky and dropped to the ground as he pulled the trigger no more than ten feet behind me. The gun went off, and a single buckshot smacked me in the back of the head as the bird dropped to the ground dead.

"We got him!" Bucky cried. "We got him!"

"Yeah, we got me, too," I said, feelin' the small wound on the back of my head. I don't think Bucky realized how close I had come to bein' a statistic. Heck, it took me a long time to figure it out. I was sleepin' one night, and the whole quail-killin' scene came up in a dream. It was then that I realized how close I'd been to becomin' a cold turkey that day. Made me break out in cold shivers.

Helen, Bucky's mom, cleaned and cooked the quail for us. The next day, just like Bucky had predicted, we were sittin' at his table, consumin' our prize.

"Be careful now," said Helen, as she passed the bird to me. "I might not have got all the buckshot out of it."

"Gee, thanks," I said.

I took a small piece and put it on my plate. I'd never eaten quail before and was a little hesitant to chow down. Slowly, I took a nibble — not bad. But then I got to thinkin' about all of the insects and worms that bird had eaten, and how it had lived out in the woods all this time, unwashed and unsupervised. I quickly lost my appetite for quail and started lookin' for somethin' else to eat. Bucky passed me what looked like brown Brussels sprouts.

"What's that?" I asked.

"Squirrel brains," said Bucky. "Have some. They're really good."

You know, Bucky's mom makes the best sliced tomatoes, potato salad, and cucumbers in the world. I just couldn't get enough of 'em that day.

After dinner, me and Bucky went for a walk back into the woods behind his house. There was a special rock back there where we sat and puzzled about the mysteries of life — our human condition, if you will. Well, we were settled-in real quiet-like on that rock, and I was wonderin' about how many pounds of worms it takes to make a pound of quail and other serious matters when the most important question of all crossed my mind.

"Bucky," I said, "how did you know yesterday that we were gonna be eatin' quail today?"

"What are you talkin' about, Johnny?"

"You know. Yesterday, before we went huntin', you told me that we were gonna eat quail."

"Lucky guess, I suppose."

"Lucky guess, my foot. Hamburgers maybe. Hot dogs, for sure. Even cold brown beans is a good guess. But quail? No way. Too far fetched."

Bucky started rubbin' his devil-catfish-bite-wound scar again and got that far-away look in his eyes.

"Johnny," he said, gazin' off into the trees, "can you keep a secret?"

"Sure."

"I can see into the future."

"Get off it, Buck. Nobody can do that."

"But I can," he said with such conviction that I almost believed him.

"You can?" I said. "Really?"

"Ever since that devil catfish bit me, all I have to do is

61

rub my scar and I can see the future. I guess ol' Be-elzebub had some kind of mental power that it used to catch its prey that got transferred to me when I got bit. At least, that's the best theory I've come up with."

"Oh, really? Well, prove it to me. What's the answers on the math test gonna be on Monday?"

"I don't know."

"But you said you could see into the future."

"Well, I can, but there's one catch. I can only see tomorrow, and I can only see what people are gonna eat. Nothin' else."

I knew then that ol' Buck was pullin' my leg. If you can see into the future, you can see into the future — not just tomorrow, and not just at supper time.

"OK then, let me give you a test. What's Clarence Caldwell gonna eat tomorrow for lunch?"

Bucky rubbed his Be-elzebub-bite-scarred hand and his eyes glazed over for a minute or two.

"RC Cola and moon pie. He's gonna get it at the fillin' station. Twelve fifteen sharp."

"Betcha a quarter."

"Johnny," said Bucky, "you just lost yourself a quarter."

The next day, we were at the fillin' station at noon with our quarters in our hands. At precisely twelve fifteen, Clarence came into the station, bought a moon pie and RC Cola, and sat down on the wall outside to trade lies with Eddie, Grit, and Hodgekins. I realized then that I had been hoodwinked. Clarence ate moon pies and RC Colas all the time. He practically lived off them, and Bucky knew that.

"Bucky, you set me up, didn't ya?" I said. "You know that Clarence lives off moon pies, don't ya?"

"Gimme your quarter, Johnny. A bet's a bet."

Reluctantly, I dropped my quarter into his hand.

"Come on," he said with a smile. "I'll take this quarter

and buy you a Coke and chips and a Milky Way." Then he added, "The time and place was the only thing I guessed, but Clarence is a pretty regular guy."

We went into the station, purchased our goods, and returned to the wall outside. We walked on past the men, sat at the end of the wall for some privacy, and started eatin' our candy bars.

"I really can see into the future," said Bucky with a big hunk of Milky Way in his mouth. "Honest."

"Sure," I said, as a piece of chocolate escaped from my mouth and fell to the ground, "and what are you gonna con me out of tomorrow?"

"Nothin'. I gave you your quarter back, didn't I?"

"Well, kinda, but — "

"Go ahead. Try me again."

"OK, what am I gonna eat for supper tomorrow?"

Bucky went through his devil-catfish-scarred-hand-rubbin' routine, and after a few minutes announced, "Blackberry cobbler, mashed potatoes, green beans, biscuits, ham, and red-eye gravy."

"You lose," I said. "Mom can't cook green beans without burnin' 'em. I haven't eaten her green beans in years."

Bucky looked me straight in the eye. It was a look that I will remember for eternity.

"Blackberry cobbler, mashed potatoes, green beans, biscuits, ham, and red-eye gravy," was all that he said.

The next day when I got home from school, Gramma Goldie was in the kitchen.

"Hi, Gramma. Where's Mom?"

"In bed, son. She's got one of those terrible migraine headaches again."

I could smell that smell that told me Gramma was cookin'. Ain't nothin' like that smell in the whole world. Never was. Never will be.

63

"What's for supper?"

"*Blackberry cobbler, mashed potatoes, green beans, biscuits, ham, and red-eye gravy,*" she said.

It was the same exact words that Bucky had uttered yesterday. From that moment on, I was a true believer. Bucky really could see into the future!

For the next two weeks, me and Bucky had a grand time with his new-found talent. Mostly, we made spendin' money by bettin' with folks at the fillin' station. But you know what? After a couple of weeks, a steady diet of Cokes and chips and Milky Ways gets kind of tiresome. Besides, bettin' like that wasn't really much fun, 'cause you always knew who was gonna win. Furthermore, it wasn't long before nobody would bet with us.

After a while, we started seein' some big flaws in Bucky's future tellin'. As we dwelt on them, we started thinkin' of Bucky as someone who was handicapped, not gifted. For one thing, you couldn't change his predictions — good or bad. If he told me I was gonna eat broccoli and cheese, well, broccoli and cheese it was. It didn't matter if we went to his house, or mine, or over to our friend Pee Wee's, the results were always the same. And another big flaw really got me frustrated.

"Bucky," I said one day as we sat on our thinkin' rock behind his house, "can't you see anything else? I mean, if you could see what our moms are fixin' for supper, then we could choose where to go each day to avoid the bad stuff."

"I don't know. I never have been able to before."

"Well, can you try again, and this time try real hard?"

Bucky squinted up his eyes and started rubbin' his devil-catfish hand.

"OK, I'll try real hard."

He squeezed his eyes real tight and grimaced up his face something awful. I thought he was gonna rub the skin off the back of his hand. After a minute or two, he collapsed back against the rock with a loud sigh.

"It's no use. It's no use. We're gonna eat cornbread and beans tomorrow, but I can't for the life of me tell you where or when."

"This is very frustratin', Bucky. If we could just get some more information along with the food, it might do some good. But just knowin' what you're gonna eat is useless. In fact, it's gettin' kind of depressin', even if you tell me I'm gonna eat something really good. It takes all of the fun — all of the excitement and anticipation out of it. And when you tell me I'm gonna eat something bad, like lima beans, there's nothin' I can do about it. It's like bein' on death row, only you just know the governor ain't gonna come through with a last minute pardon, if you know what I mean. I think I'd rather not know at all."

"Yeah," agreed Bucky, "I get the same feelin'. But, Johnny, we can't give up. How many people do you know who can tell the future?"

I didn't know of any except ol' Buck, but then, maybe lots of people could see the future, and they just weren't tellin' me about it. Granny seemed to have the knack for predictin' when folks' fortunes were gonna change. She was always makin' predictions about how so-and-so was headed for trouble and, sure enough, within a couple of days, poor so-and-so was neck deep in it. And then there were my teachers who were always tellin' me how worthless I was gonna be when I grow up. So far, they had been right on target. Makes ya wonder, doesn't it?

"If we can find a way to increase my power," continued Bucky, "who knows what we can do."

"You're right, Bucky. You're absolutely right. But what do you think we should do?"

"Go seinin' for minnows in Scrapper's Sink Hole," he

65

said without hesitation.

"Ain't no way."

"Yeah, we got to. If we can catch ol' Be-elzebub again and get it to bite me again, maybe it will give me more powers. And if we keep it locked up, then we can get it to bite you, too."

"Bucky, you're talkin' nonsense," I said. "Another bite from that thing might kill ya. And, besides, you're not sure that it was the bite that did it in the first place."

"Oh, I'm pretty sure all right."

"How come?" I asked.

"Cause I've been havin' visions of giant sea bass swimmin' in a vast underground ocean."

(To be honest with you, folks, I was never totally at ease bein' alone with Bucky after that.)

Well, me and Bucky wallowed the problem around for several more days. We tried every angle we could think of to squeeze more information out of Bucky's prognostications. All we got was frustration. Bucky kept insistin' that we go and try catchin' that devil catfish again. And I kept resistin'. Finally, things came to a head. We were back on our thinkin' rock gettin' ready to try another forecast. This time Bucky made an interestin' and scary prediction.

"Footlong hot dog and a chocolate milkshake."

"Yes!" I said, throwin' a victorious fist in the air. "Dad's takin' me to Tom's Carry Out tomorrow."

"Nope. That was for me. I'm havin' a footlong and a milkshake. You're havin' nothin'."

"You mean you can't tell what I'm havin'?"

"No. I can see what you're gonna eat tomorrow, and it's nothin'. You're not eatin' anything tomorrow. Nothin.' All day. No breakfast, no lunch, no dinner."

"But can't I go to Tom's Carry Out with you tomorrow? I promise I'll pay for my own hot dog."

"Johnny, you know I only make the predictions. I can't change them or stop them."

"But what does that mean: I'm not eatin'?"

"Well, maybe you get sick, or — "

"Or maybe I get dead. Or maybe I get run over by a truck, or a fire burns down my house and kills my whole family — Bucky, what's my Mom and Dad eatin' tomorrow?"

"Footlong hot dogs and chocolate milkshakes."

"That means I am dead! They'd never go to Tom's without me if I was alive." I paused to think about the logic of the situation. "That means I'm dead, and they're celebratin' with you! Bucky, you've got to promise me if I die tomorrow, you won't go to Tom's Carry Out with Mom and Dad and celebrate."

"Why should I promise that?"

"Cause then I won't die, that's why. Don't you see the logic — "

"You're talkin' plum nonsense, Johnny. You're not gonna die."

"Well, I have no plans for fastin', so why am I not eatin' tomorrow?"

"Don't know."

Then an idea popped into my head — the devil catfish.

"Bucky, we've got to catch that devil catfish, and get him to bite you again, and maybe then we can figure out a way to change the future. That's our only hope. — That's my only hope."

Bucky didn't need any more encouragement because he'd been wantin' to catch ol' Be-elzebub all along. So, off we raced with our net to Scrapper's Sink Hole. We splashed around for fifteen minutes or so and didn't even catch a minnow.

"Wait a minute, Johnny. We've got to calm down or

67

we'll never catch anything. Now close your eyes and concentrate all of your thoughts on ol' Be-elzebub, that scoundrel of a devil catfish — ol' deer guts himself — the key to
our future fame and fortune."

And so we stood real still in the creek for a minute or
two, eyes closed, tryin' to harmonize our thoughts with nature, tryin' to conjure up ol' Be-elzebub.

Finally, Bucky said, "OK, now, Johnny, real slow and
easy-like."

We practically tiptoed around the edges of the sink
hole, our arms shakin' in anticipation. Something just told
me we were gonna be successful. And sure enough, there
came a sudden tug on the net, and when we lifted it up, ol'
Be-elzebub had returned. Bucky started to shout in triumph
when old deer guts suddenly transformed into legs and tails
and teeth. It made a wild leap and bit me right on the nose!

I don't remember much after that. All I know is there
was a terrible pain in my nose, and everything went black.
I woke up two days later in the hospital. Mom and Dad and
Bucky were smilin' down at me when I woke up. Mom
lifted me up off the bed and gave me a hug so hard that it
almost made me pass out again. Dad smiled and patted my
head, and Bucky just stood there with a stupid look on his
face like he was the gladdest person in the world to see me.
We talked for a little while, and they told me how long I
had been unconscious. Mom said the doctor said the wound
on my nose should heal up pretty good, and, for a boy, it
shouldn't effect my looks too much.

Just before they were ready to leave, Bucky asked to
talk to me in private. Mom and Dad went into the hall,
leavin' me and Bucky all alone in the room.

"Well, Johnny, you didn't die."

"Nope, but I guess I came close."

"You certainly did." Bucky paused as if deep in

thought. "You know, Johnny, I think we ought to give up tryin' to predict the future. Just between you and me, it's not worth it. I mean, we got so worried about tomorrow that we plum forgot about today. But when I saw you lyin' there, nearly dead, I realized how unimportant tomorrow really is. It's today that counts. So no more of this stupid predictin', OK?"

I reached out and shook his hand.

"OK, Bucky. Here's to today. Let tomorrow worry about itself."

Bucky turned to leave.

"Wait a minute," I said. "What about the footlong hot dogs and milkshakes?"

"Well, after we brought you up to the hospital, I was blamin' myself so much for what had happened that your Mom and Dad took me to Tom's to try and cheer me up."

"So, that's how it happened."

"Yep, that's how it happened," Bucky said. "And oh, by the way, I will make one last prediction. You ain't gonna like the food here."

"Why not?"

"Do you know how this hospital came to be? It was originally a cafeteria, and one day the owner said, 'The food is so bad here, we might as well turn this place into a hospital.'"

I laughed. When I did, I started to cough and wheeze somethin' terrible.

"Bucky, can you hand me a tissue?"

"Sure."

As I started to blow my nose, an irresistible urge came over me. I leaned back in the bed, closed my eyes, and continued to rub the devil-catfish wound on my nose.

"Blue jeans and a red flannel shirt," I announced.

"What?" said Bucky.

"Blue jeans and a red flannel shirt. I can see the future, Bucky, just like you, and that's what you're gonna be wearin' tomorrow."

To this day, I've never had the heart to tell him that I was just kiddin'.

The Black Winds of October

I'll make a bet with you. In most stories, quaint villages are always associated with witchcraft and evil. Check it out yourself. The next time you see a story about a small, backwoods hamlet on television or at the movies, I bet it will be part of a horror story or supernatural tale. You know what I'm talking about. A young couple stumbles onto a picture-perfect old town. All the houses look like something out of a Colonial American history book. And all of the people are beautiful and friendly. The young couple falls in love with the place and decides to move in. Terrible decision. After a few days of peaceful bliss, they accidentally uncover the horrible fact that they are living in the midst of (take your pick) vampires, Satan worshipers, witches, zombies, or werewolves. And the ring leader is always the local sheriff, pastor, or doctor — someone the young couple would trust with their lives.

In one version of the story, the couple gets tortured or eaten alive. In the other version, the young couple manages to escape and burns down the town, killing all of the vampires, Satan worshipers, witches, zombies, or werewolves. Of course, one of the evil things escapes and moves to the big city until it can start all over again in another remote part of the world. I'm sure you've seen that plot repeated a hundred times. It's a plot that does a great disservice to quaint, rural towns, not to mention all of the preachers,

71

doctors, and sheriffs who labor therein.

Well, I have a story to tell about a small, remote mountain hamlet that I stumbled upon several years ago. It was not populated by vampires and such, but by honest, decent, caring people. And yet, there is a horror story to tell here also — one greater than any demon you might imagine. But I get ahead of myself with the story.

My adventure began on a morning in mid-autumn. As was my custom, I was deep in the Appalachians in the midst of my annual mountain hunting trip. I was never much of a hunter, but I always enjoyed the solitude of the mountains, especially in autumn with the leaves in full color. I also made a firm practice of hunting alone, away from the gangs of other hunters. They were much too noisy for my liking.

That fateful day of discovery began with a clear, bright October morning. As I made my way slowly from my camp to the distant mountain crest, the temperature was about sixty degrees with a promise of reaching the seventies by afternoon. The weather was perfect for hiking, and I walked along paying more attention to the scenery than to where I was going. The trees were still heavy with leaves, creating a canopy which blocked out most of the sunlight on the forest floor. An occasional flurry of wind would move the trees just enough to allow the sunlight to dance through the underbrush, revealing a dazzling array of fresh-fallen foliage. I soon decided to forgo the hunting and dedicated the day to exploration and sightseeing.

By noon, I was resting on the mountaintop which had earlier seemed so far away. As I sat munching on a peanut butter sandwich and contemplating the mountains, I noticed a blackness in the west — apparently, swirling clouds of rain. A storm was approaching. This was not unusual for this time of year. In the midst of changing seasons, the weather could change three or four times a day, shifting from bright sunlight to black, angry rain squalls. But this storm caught me completely by surprise. At first, I watched as it rolled over the mountains on the horizon, devouring each one in its path as it approached. It was mesmerizing to watch, but my attention quickly shifted when I began to realize that this was a fast-moving storm and would soon overtake the mountain on which I sat. It was time for me to head home.

I could not, however, outrun the storm. Within minutes, it was swirling around me. The wind was whipping around so hard that the blowing leaves stung my face and hands. A large tree cracked and fell close by, convincing me to take shelter under a nearby rock ledge. For about an hour — it seemed much longer — I sat in relative safety as the storm ripped through the forest around me. There was no rain, but the sky grew increasingly dark, and the whole forest was in motion. Trees were bending low, struggling to keep from being uprooted. The leaves were being driven with such force that at one point I was almost covered with them as they blew across the rock ledge. There was nothing for me to do but to wait it out. And wait I did.

When the wind storm passed, I was confronted with a new problem. A dense fog had settled-in, making it impossible to see any landmarks. I should have stayed under that rock ledge, but I didn't. When nightfall descended sooner than I expected and blackness overtook the fog, I realized that I was hopelessly disoriented. In short, I was lost. That night a steady, gentle rain began to fall.

The night was spent under another rock ledge. (Or perhaps it was the same one. Who could tell?) I did not notice being wet and cold. I was too preoccupied with listening for some sound to give me direction. My ears strained for the noise of a distant car, or a train, or human voice — or even a gunshot. But except for water dripping from the leaves and an occasional deer or possum, I heard nothing.

The following morning, the fog was still thick on the mountain. Surely, by noon it will lift, I thought, and I will be able to get my bearings and find my way out. But noon came and went and the fog remained. Impatiently, I began to wander aimlessly, yelling into the fog in hopes that I would stumble into a rescue. It never occurred to me that if I found anyone else in this forest of fog that they would probably be just as lost as I was. By the second nightfall, I was too tired to sit and listen. Burrowing into the leaves, I quickly fell asleep.

There is not much to tell about the third day except that it was a repeat of the second. I had been in the mountains many times before, but I had never experienced such a persistent fog. I was totally unprepared to deal with it. I did find some hickory nuts to eat, but most of the day was spent wandering in the fog and hoping against hope that I would be discovered. As the day wore on, I became acutely aware of just how cold and tired I had become. I also became resigned to the fact that I was lost indefinitely and had to take better measures to protect myself. By nightfall of the third day, I had fashioned a lean-to against another rock ledge and had managed to accumulate enough dry leaves for more comfortable sleeping quarters. I had brought matches, but they were back at my base camp — somewhere out there in the fog.

Yes, somewhere out there in the fog was my tent. My mind began to think of the absurd. My tent and safety could be miles away. Or it could be a few feet away. I had heard a story once about a man who was trapped in his truck during a snowstorm in the mountains of Colorado. He was on one of those roads that are closed and do not get cleared in the winter. Somehow he had the misfortune of being on the mountain when a storm hit. Consequently, the road was closed for the season. The poor man never left his truck, but waited patiently to be rescued. But the rescue never came and he starved to death — right there in the middle of the road. The snowplow crew found him the next spring when they came through. He was only a hundred yards around the curve from the point where the plows turned around during the winter. A hundred yards. He could have left his truck and walked to safety in five minutes if he had only known in which direction to go.

The next morning I was awakened by a gentle tapping on my left shoulder. I opened my eyes to be greeted by a stocky middle-aged man carrying an oak walking stick. He was about five-foot ten and built like a barrel from head to foot. His arms bulged from his white shirt, and his legs looked as if they were going to split open his black pants at any moment. His face was clean shaven, and his skin, smooth, taunt and shiny, framed a broad smile and friendly eyes. His hairline showed only a hint of baldness, and his cheeks glowed red in the cool mountain air. He peered down at me and chuckled.

"Well, Pilgrim, you look like ya might be having a bit-a-trouble." He trilled his 'r's with a distinct Scottish accent.

"I'm lost, I think," I said.

"And hungry, I suspect."

"Yes, very."

He had two small pouches on his belt. There was a black one on his right side and a brown one on his left. Reaching into the black pouch, he pulled out a small loaf of bread with a hunk of cheese and handed them to me.

"Then you'll be a-needin' these, I suspect."

That was my first encounter with Squire Hoose. Looking back, I wish it had been my last.

After normal introductions, Squire Hoose sat down on

the protruding roots of a nearby tree and waited patiently as I devoured the bread and cheese. As I ate, I explained my situation, and as I listened to myself recount my story, I became more and more embarrassed by my foolishness. The weather was once again clear and bright, only accentuating the fact that my lost condition had been only temporary. On a day like this, I thought, I could surely find my way home, even without the good Mr. Hoose's help.

As I downed the last piece of bread, he said, "Well, I suppose that you'll be a-needin' to shed those wet clothes."

"Yes," I said, "and a little help in finding my way back to my campsite."

"In due time, me lad," he said, looking around. "But first things first. Let's get you into the village." He arose and looked at me. "Are you strong enough to walk?"

At first, the question struck me as a little insulting. After all, I had only been in the woods for three days, and I had found some nuts to sustain me. But when I realized that he was genuinely concerned for my health and safety, the emotion passed.

"Sure," I said. "Lead the way."

We walked for perhaps an hour through the woods, crossing several ridge lines along the way. Whenever the opportunity presented itself, I tried to identify some landmark — a mountain peak or a distinct hollow — that would give me some clue to where I was. At one point, we stopped on the crest of a ridge, and Squire showed me an overlook of the valley below. We were standing on an outcropping of rock that allowed an unobstructed view. None of the mountains looked familiar to me. Nothing could be seen except a sea of colors beneath a deep blue autumn sky.

"Where are we?" I asked.

"Cromwell. It's right down there below us."

I inspected the valley below, but could not see a town.

"Where?" I asked.

"Down there," he replied, pointing to a hollow that ran up to the right of where we were standing.

As I followed his finger, I could finally see the hint of a house or two, but nothing more.

"Must be a small community," I said.

"Couple hundred, give or take you and me," he said with a wink. "Come on now, Paul, we've got to get off this mountain or we'll be late for lunch!"

Continuing our trek, we descended quietly through the red and yellow foliage along a narrow path that clung to a steep and oft' times rocky slope. I could imagine snake problems along this path in the summer. Finally, emerging from the trees, we came face to face with the back side of Squire's house. It came into view so suddenly, emerging from the surrounding trees, that I felt as if it had sprung up from the forest floor.

"Well, there she be, me lad — the Hoose house. Come on in and we'll see what Rebecca's been a-cookin' for us."

The house was a two-story colonial, complete with white clapboard siding, black shutters, and no less than three dormers. The backyard was just a small, leaf-covered clearing. The trees surrounded the house in such a fashion that no other houses were visible.

A back window was open, and coming from that window was a smell made in heaven. Rebecca was baking a turkey and its aroma, enhanced by the sage and other spices, was delicious beyond belief. At that moment in my life, there was nothing I wanted more than to sit down to dinner with Squire Hoose and his family. And dine we did. It was beyond my expectations. I have never tasted a meal anymore delicious or satisfying than what Rebecca served up that day. Of course, my hunger probably had a lot to do with that opinion. And subsequent meals — of which there were several — were only enhanced by the memory of the first one.

Before dinner, Squire found some dry clothes for me to wear — black and white — no colors. The furniture in the house was simple, yet elegant. The decorations were sparse, and I saw no evidence of an electrical appliance. I decided they must be Amish or some other denomination like that, but as a guest and stranger, I felt it improper to discuss religion with them.

After dinner, Squire insisted I tour the community with him. He seemed eager to show me all that Cromwell had to offer. I was so taken by his hospitality that I almost forgot I was lost.

"Squire, before we go," I said, "do you have a phone so I can call my family and tell them I'm all right?"

"We have no phones here in Cromwell."

"None?"

"None. Oh, we know about your phones and televisions. But we have none here in Cromwell. We have no need for them."

"Don't you ever want to contact your friends and family who live somewhere else?"

"Why would they live anywhere else but in Cromwell, Paul? Come, let me show you what I mean."

As we started for the door, Rebecca came running from the kitchen.

"Don't forget your pouches Squire," she said, handing him the black and brown leather pouches I had noticed earlier when we had first met. "And Paul needs some, too," she said.

She opened a cedar chest and rummaged through it, emerging with two pouches and a belt. She handed them to me. They appeared to be empty.

"The black one goes on the right and the brown one on

78

the left," she said seriously.

"What are these for?" I asked.

Squire's cheeks glowed as he smiled that broad smile of his. "You'll find out soon enough, me lad. You'll find out soon enough."

We walked outside and stood on the front porch that ran the length of the house. The porch was lined with a white banister that, coupled with the surrounding trees, seemed to frame the street in front of us like a picture. A single, small, cobblestone street ran though the town, winding past houses and stores that were constructed in much the same manner as the Hoose house. All of the buildings were nestled into the trees with only the front part of each structure visible from the street. Toward the north end of the street, young children, dressed in black and white, were playing kickball and jump rope. A couple of horses were tied in front of "Ott's Hardware." Most of the people, of which there were several, could be seen walking or standing in groups of twos and threes along the road. The little hamlet was a-buzz with activity.

"Come," said Squire, "let's go visit the bakery."

"But we just ate."

"Never rest on your laurels," said Squire, patting his substantial belly.

We stepped from the porch onto the street, and I had the strangest feeling that I was stepping into a different world. Almost immediately, several people stopped their activities and peered my way. I guess it wasn't hard to recognize a stranger in this small town. A silence quickly spread through the street. And that's when it happened.

A small girl, perhaps seven or eight, who had been playing nearby, dropped her jump rope and ran up to me. She was wearing a long, black dress, and she had long, blonde hair that was tied into pigtails on each side of her head. As she ran, I could see her little black shoes and white socks appear and disappear from under her dress. She stopped directly in front of me and looked straight into my eyes, demanding eye contact in return. She then reached into the brown pouch hanging from the left side of her belt and pulled something out. Her fist was clinched, and I could not see what was in her hand. She extended her hand to me, and her face broke into a big smile as she said, "The top of the day to you, Pilgrim Stranger."

I stood looking at the girl, not knowing what to do.

"Take her gift," whispered Squire.

Obediently, I extended my open palm. Gleefully, she raised her clinched fist and dropped her offering into my hand. It was a gold coin!

"Now put it in your brown pouch," instructed Squire with another whisper.

"But —"

"No 'buts', just do as I say," Squire said through the side of his mouth as he smiled and nodded to the crowd.

I wondered how I could I accept such a gift from a complete stranger. But then I glanced at all of the eyes that were fixed upon me. If this was one of their customs, it was certainly an expensive one.

"Thank you," I said, as I placed the gold coin in my pouch. And then, as an afterthought, "And the top of the day to you, too —"

"Sarah," the girl said.

"Sarah," I repeated. "And the top of the day to you, too, Sarah."

Everyone seemed to be pleased with that exchange and promptly went back to their business. It was as if I had been officially accepted as a member of their community and no further introductions or evaluations needed to be made.

"And now, on to the bakery," announced Squire.

"Whoa, wait a minute, Squire," I said, throwing up my hands in protest. "I need an explanation. That little girl just gave me a gold coin."

"It was just a trifle, Paul."

"A what? A trifle, did you say?"

"Yes. Often, when we greet people, we give them a trifle, a token of our friendship."

"But I wouldn't call a gold coin a 'trifle'. Couldn't this custom get a little expensive? Especially if you don't get many in return?"

Squire reached into his black bag and pulled out a piece of cheese. He reached into his brown pouch and pulled out a gold coin. "Tell me, Paul, when you were up there on the mountain — cold and lost — which one of these would have been more important to you?"

I was sorely tempted, but answered, "Why, the cheese, of course."

"Correct. When a man is lost, alone, and hungry, gold means nothing to him." Squire put the cheese back into his pouch. He handed the coin to me. "And when a man's belly is full, and he's surrounded by friends, he has no need for gold, either. The top of the day to ya, me lad."

Rather dumbfounded, I placed the coin into my pouch and followed Squire, who was hastily making his way down the street toward the bakery.

Katie Morgan was busily arranging her fresh-baked bread on the counter when Squire and I arrived at the bakery. Katie looked up from her work, smiled, and greeted us.

"Well, good day to you, Squire. Who's your new friend?"

"This is Paul, Paul Schoolcraft. He's come to visit — a bit by accident I might add."

"Oh, I see," she said. Extending her hand, she added, "Welcome to Cromwell, Paul. Make yourself at home." I shook her hand as she turned her attention to Squire. "And what will it be for you today, Squire?"

Squire surveyed the goodies, rubbing his hands, his eyes wide open with delight like a three-year-old. After much deliberation, he said, "I believe Paul and I will have a sampling of those cinnamon-sprinkled apple turnovers. Three for me and — " he looked me over from head to foot as if trying to size-up my eating capacity. "And one for me friend, Paul. I think that'll do."

"Coffee?"

"Yes, that will do fine."

Gathering our bounty, we sat down in the corner at a small wooden table. Squire launched into his first turnover with great gusto.

"Mmmmmm, apple and cinnamon. A match made in heaven."

I nibbled on my turnover. It was good — extremely good — but I was more interested in watching Katie Morgan's clientele. People were coming and going constantly, and a curious pattern arose. Katie always filled their orders with great speed and accuracy, but she never wrote anything down. In fact, she never rang up any sales on the cash register. Some people gave her a gold coin from their brown pouch. But some simply took their goods and, after a minute or two of conversation, left without paying for anything. Another curious thing was that everything cost the same. I never saw Katie give any change in return.

"Squire, have you noticed something curious going on here?" I asked.

"Like what?"

"Have you noticed that half of the people don't pay for their food?"

"What's so unusual about that? If Katie wants to give away her stuff, like she did to you and me, that's her business. Furthermore, if people want to give her a trifle or two, then that's theirs."

"But she can't stay in business operating that way," I insisted.

"She's been doing it for forty-seven years. Hasn't had any problems yet."

We sat at the table for another twenty minutes at least, and the pattern did not change. Some people paid, and some people didn't. And the people who paid were not in the least bit upset. I struggled in my mind to understand this strange, yet charming, economy. At last Squire finished off his third turnover and fourth cup of coffee.

"Ready to continue your tour?" he asked, rising to leave.

"But we haven't paid for this."

"Does that bother you?"

"Yes."

"Then offer Katie a trifle or two."

I reached into my pouch and pulled out a coin. It looked like an awful lot to pay for a few turnovers and coffee.

"The top of the day to you, Katie Morgan," I said, handing her the coin.

"Why, thank you, Paul," she said, placing my coin in her pouch. "And the top of the day to you, too."

As Squire and I left the bakery, I felt the warmest glow course through my body. Somehow, I sensed it wasn't the apple turnover.

The rest of the afternoon was spent visiting Ott's Hardware, Mabel's Grocery, and Samuel's Blacksmith Shop. The people were simply enchanting. We spent an hour at Ott's talking about how to rejuvenate an old, rusty water pump and another at Mabel's sampling the plums. (Squire did most of the sampling.) Mabel expounded upon the value of growing herbs in the kitchen window sill. Ac-

83

cording to Mabel, herbs not only provided a ready source of cooking spices, but they also prevented what she called 'huburus' from accumulating in your house. I had no idea what 'huburus' was, but by the way Mabel talked about it, it was definitely something to be avoided at all costs.

Curiously, the method of payment at all of these stores was the same. Pay if you want and one coin buys all. And strangely, much to my delight, all along the way, total strangers would greet me and offer me a trifle. At the end of the afternoon, I had accumulated quite a number. At this rate, I could see staying on a few more days and returning from my lost adventure a very rich man.

That evening Squire, Rebecca, and I sat under dim candlelight at their dinner table. We had been talking about nothing in particular when I reached for my pouch and poured its contents onto the table.

"What are you doing?" asked Rebecca in surprise. She sounded offended.

"Why, I'm going to count my coins," I said.

"Oh, no, Paul," said Squire, placing his hand over the pile. "You must never count your trifles. Never."

"But how will you know when you're running out?"

"You will never run out," Squire said emphatically. "Never."

"But if someone gives away more than they get, they have to run out eventually," I insisted. "You have to count them to know how many you can afford to give away."

"No one ever counts," declared Rebecca.

"And no one ever runs out," said Squire. "Now put them back in your pouch. And never, never count them!"

That night I pondered the events of the day. That morning I had been hungry, wet, cold, and lost on a nameless mountain. Tonight I was among the warmest, friendliest people I had ever met — and the strangest people I had ever met. I lay in bed trying to understand their unique way of doing business, but it was beyond me. No matter how I tried to run the numbers or figure the statistics, it didn't add up. Sooner or later, someone was going to get greedy and accumulate the wealth of the entire town in one, big, enormous, brown pouch. Then what were these poor, naive folks going to do?

Another possibility crossed my mind. Perhaps, I had died and gone to heaven. Yes, that was it. I was in heaven. But then Stephen King crossed my mind. You know Stephen King, the horror-story writer. There were plenty of stories about hamlets like this where nothing was as it seemed. Why, at this very moment, Katie Morgan was probably transforming into a werewolf, or bat, or some unspeakably hideous creature. A creature destined to prowl the night, looking for some unsuspecting soul like me, with his belly full of apple turnovers, to devour. Perhaps by tomorrow, I would be *in* the apple turnovers. Perhaps Squire Hoose, the owner of this very guest room in which I slept, was the ring leader. Perhaps he, too, was metamorphosing into a monster at that very moment. I covered my head with my pillow and tried not to think about it.

The following morning, I awoke, still in one piece and still quite alive. I inspected my neck for puncture marks. There were none. I inspected the rest of my body for signs of strange rashes or any other unusual telltale marks. Again, I had a clean bill of health. Perhaps, I thought, Squire is going to fatten me up a bit before moving in for the kill.

However, during breakfast with Squire and Rebecca, all thoughts of werewolves and vampires quickly melted away. The conversation was light and cheery, and Squire and Rebecca were so gracious that thoughts of any devious plot against me seemed impossible. Rebecca was a consummate host, and her obvious devotion to Squire only added to her charm. There was no question about who ruled the household operations. It was clearly Rebecca, and Squire honored her position without question. She moved with grace throughout the house, a place where she plainly ruled without being overbearing.

After breakfast, Squire and I spent the rest of the morning chopping wood to stockpile for the winter. After another hearty lunch, we visited Katie's bakery again. This time it was for the cherry tarts. And this time, Squire gave Katie two trifles. All throughout the afternoon, people continued to greet me and give me gold coins, trifles as they called them. Mentally, I tried to keep count not only of the number of coins, but also their value. Based on the current price of gold and the weight of the coins, I calculated that I had accumulated tens of thousands of dollars. Returning to my guest room, I stored all but a few of the coins in a drawer beside my bed, but I did not, as Squire had warned, actually count them. I put the few remaining coins back into my pouch.

I found myself late that afternoon sitting on a small rock wall that lined the north end of the street leading out of town. I was trying to decide how long I was going to stay and how much money I could accumulate before leaving. As I was pondering my spoils, Sarah, the little girl who had so generously greeted me the day before, came skipping down the street. Seeing me, she ran over, sat down beside me, and offered me another trifle. Being polite (and not wishing to take advantage of her) I offered her one in return. She was a sweet little girl, and we sat on the wall, talking about her dolls and other playthings. I soon discovered she had only two flaws. She was too trusting of strangers, and she insisted on giving everybody who came along one of her trifles.

Only last week, I had read in the newspaper about a little girl about Sarah's age who had been abducted and — the thought of what had happened was too horrible for me to contemplate. A shiver went down my spine as I looked at Sarah as she innocently kicked her heals against the wall. Suppose, I thought, some stranger should wander into town — a stranger intent upon doing evil — and Sarah fell into his hands. What if — .

"Sarah, do you always greet strangers the way you did me yesterday?"

"Sure, why not?"

"Because, Sarah, some people are not like me. Some people want to hurt little girls like you."

"Why would anyone want to do that?"

"That's just the way the world is," I said, realizing that I had started a conversation that I was not prepared to finish. Besides, it was her parent's responsibility to tell her these things. "Just be careful who you talk to, Sarah. You shouldn't be giving your trifles to just anyone."

Sarah furrowed her brow, thinking about the advice I had just given her.

"And another thing," I said, smiling and trying to change the conversation, "you will run out of trifles if you give them to everybody who comes along."

"Will not."

"Oh, yes, you will."

"Haven't yet."

I was determined to explain to someone, anyone, the logic of my assertion. "Look, I'll show you. See my pouch? I have trifles in it, right?"

"Right."

"Now watch this."

As people came by, I began to give each one a trifle from my already depleted pouch. Some I gave two. In just a few minutes, my pouch was empty. I came back, sat down beside Sarah on the wall, and turned my pouch inside out.

"There," I said triumphantly, "it's empty."

Sarah looked at my pouch for what seemed a long time in disbelief. And then without saying a word, she jumped down from the wall and ran down the street. "Mommy" is all I could hear her crying.

I stayed for two more days in Cromwell, accumulating coins and helping Squire Hoose around his house. To be honest, I was enjoying myself so much I almost forgot I had a family back there "in the other world" that probably thought I was dead. The attraction to stay in Cromwell and its peaceful way of life was strong, but an upcoming event started to make me nervous and wary. Everybody in town started talking about their annual Fall Festival Bonfire, and Ott and Katie insisted that I be the special guest of honor. When I asked what would be involved, all they could tell me was I would truly be surprised. Once again, visions of werewolves or twisted Satan worshipers began to haunt me at night. And when the town folk started piling kindling up in the middle of the street, I knew I needed to make my escape. I discussed my planned departure with Squire, who was soundly disappointed with my decision.

"Well, I hate the thought of you missing the bonfire, Paul. We had such a great surprise planned for you. But I guess it is best for you to return and let your family know you are all right. Of course, you are welcome to come back and visit us, but only at certain times."

"Oh, really?" I asked.

"I shall escort you from town, but you must only return during the black winds of October."

I thought Squire was growing a bit mysterious — "the black winds of October?" What was that?

"Promise me," he insisted.

"I promise, Squire, but how will you know when I'm coming back?"

"Trust me, me lad, I will know." He glanced toward Rebecca who nodded. "Now, let's prepare for your departure."

I was allowed no good-byes with the town folks. Instead, we packed a few provisions, and Squire and I left through his backdoor along the same path that had originally lead us into town. We climbed through the mountains until we came to the lean-to that I had constructed several days earlier. Squire stopped and put down his sack.

"I must leave you here, Paul. You can stay here for the night. There's a sleeping bag in the pack."

"But I don't know where I am," I protested.

"You will in the morning. I promise."

The winds began to stir, and the sky in the west began to darken.

"The black winds are coming again, Paul. I must be going. Now promise me you'll stay right here."

"I promise," I said, not understanding what was happening.

Squire shook my hand, and headed back along the path to the village. Within an hour, the winds were blowing fiercely, forcing me to take refuge in the lean-to. While the winds blew, I rolled out my sleeping bag, and in the dark, poured out the contents of my trifle pouch. The count came to 137 — 137 gold coins. I could not calculate their worth. I scooped them up and placed them back in the pouch, tucking it safely under my sleeping bag.

The winds howled most of the night, but when I awoke in the morning, the autumn sun was once again shining brightly. I emerged from the lean-to and looked around. The woods looked strangely different. I could no longer find the path to Cromwell, and I was soon confronted with another huge disappointment. The pouch was gone. I torn the lean-to apart and cleared the leaves in a twenty-foot circle, but there was no pouch to be found. Perhaps Squire had come back in the night and "retrieved" it while I had slept. Perhaps Squire and the whole town of Cromwell had been just a dream, an hallucination. Perhaps I had been lying in a stupor for days — weak and dehydrated — and had imagined the whole thing. It was critical, now that I had regained my senses, to find my way home. This time luck was with me. In just a few minutes, I topped the crest of a nearby ridge and immediately recognized a landmark. I knew where I was. Within a couple of hours, I came out of the woods at Johnson's filling station. I was only a few miles from where I had originally become lost.

I told no one about my visit with Squire Hoose and the village of Cromwell. A little research uncovered no mention of Cromwell as a town in the area. I could not find it on any map. Perhaps I had been dreaming all along.

A year passed, and October came again. Cromwell had, indeed, faded like a dream as I got back into the grind of daily life. But as the leaves turned again and the autumn breezes began to blow, something stirred inside me. I felt compelled to attempt a return visit to Squire Hoose, if for nothing more than to prove that he was only a dream. And then I remembered his instructions — the black winds of October. What could he mean? Why, storms, of course. I must return during the storms of October.

I watched the weather forecasts to time my return. When the time looked ripe, I set off for the mountains. I returned to the spot of my lean-to, which I quickly rebuilt. This time I was prepared with food and shelter. On the second day, the sky began to darken, and the winds began to roll across the ridges. Once again, like the first storm a year earlier, there was no rain, just howling winds and a deep darkness, followed by an extended fog. On the fourth day, like clockwork, the fog lifted, and the good-natured Squire Hoose appeared walking along the path!

We repeated our trek into town, and Rebecca's turkey dinner, and our trip to Katie's bakery. Everything seemed to be exactly as I had left it. Perhaps I was dreaming, I thought. If so, my dream was about to take an unexpected turn. On the second day in town, I became curious. I had been looking for the little girl, Sarah, but she was not with the other children. Finally that evening as we sat around the kitchen table, I inquired about her.

"She's dead," said Rebecca.

"Dead?" I repeated in disbelief. A view of her entered my mind — young, innocent, and full of life. It was hard to imagine her any other way.

"Yes," said Squire, "she's dead."

"But . . . but what happened? An accident?"

"No one knows," said Rebecca. "Her mother said she came home one day — about a month after you left — mumbled something silly about her pouch being empty, which everybody knows is impossible, and went into a deep melancholy. A depression. Refused to eat, poor child, and soon withered away and died."

Tears welled in my eyes at the story. An uneasy feeling settled into my soul. Her death was disturbing, very disturbing.

"But she's at peace now," said Squire.

The words were of little comfort to me.

I stayed several more days in Cromwell. Everything appeared to go on unchanged from my first visit. The people were still friendly, the economy was still the same, and trifles flowed apparently as freely as before. But Sarah's death had taken the edge off the whole experience. During the last two days of my visit, I became depressed. I refused to accept people's trifles and even began to shun Squire's good-natured company. What good were the trifles anyway? I would be leaving soon and all of my trifles would have to be left behind again like the first time. They could keep their trifles for all I cared. However, each time I refused a trifle, the town folks became more and more shocked and confused. They simply could not understand why anyone would refuse a trifle. I was more than eager to explain my actions and share my melancholy with anyone who would listen.

Squire soon sensed my disposition and realized the discord I was spreading throughout the town. He suggested that perhaps my visit should end. I agreed. Nevertheless, he offered a return visit — next year during the black winds. I did not tell him that I wasn't so sure I wanted to come back.

But come back I did, although it took me three years to do so. It wasn't because I did not try. It was because for three years the black winds refused to blow. On the third year of trying, however, the winds, blackness, and fog returned. But when the fog lifted, Squire Hoose was not there to greet me. Instead, Ott, the hardware man, came hurrying up the path. A worried look was on his face.

"Squire? Is he OK?" I asked.

"Oh, he's fine all right, but he didn't feel like comin' to get ya. Told me to run on up here, so we'd better hurry. I got a store to run and every hour means lost business."

Ott's comment shocked me. It was completely out of character for him. In the times I had met him, he was an easy going, genial person. Today he was gruff and agitated. We hurried along the path to town, arriving via a slightly different route at Ott's backdoor.

"Squire's home waitin' on ya," Ott said gruffly, "and I've got to get back to work. See ya later."

Ott disappeared through his back door, leaving me

alone in his backyard. I opened the door and followed him into his store to gain access to the street. Immediately, I knew something was terribly wrong in Cromwell. Hanging in Ott's storefront window was a sign that declared "ABSOLUTELY NO CREDIT." I hurried on to Squire's house to find out what was going on. I knocked on the door and Rebecca answered. She was not smiling. She took me to the kitchen where I found Squire sitting with his elbows on the table, his head resting in his hands. When I entered the room, he did not look up.

"Top of the day to you, Squire," I said.

"Oh, yeah? Well, what's so good about it?"

The color was gone from his normally rosy cheeks. I sat down beside him, realizing he was despondent.

"Squire, we've got to talk. There's something terribly wrong here. I just came from Ott's, and he's charging for all of his goods."

"That's not the half of it," said Squire. "Katie's quit making her cinnamon-apple turnovers. She told me that they were much too expensive and she was loosing money on them."

"That cannot be true."

"Oh, but it is," said Squire. "I'm quite afraid that it is."

He proceeded to tell me of the events of the last three years. Shortly after I left, a few of the town folks came up with empty trifle pouches, creating quite a stir. There was an ugly town meeting where accusations of thievery, dishonesty, and shady dealings were aired. Some people claimed the problem was that people just didn't care enough. Other people claimed there was too much greed. The problem would go away for a few months, but it would always return. And when it did return, it was always worse than the time before. Some proposed doing away with trifles altogether. Others took a moral high ground and argued that the folks who were running out of trifles just weren't living right. Squire was one of those who had taken such a stand, roundly condemning those who were abandoning the trifle tradition.

"Paul," Squire said with a woeful look in his eyes, "I believed all along that I was right. I fought for the old traditions that I knew worked. But this morning when I went to give a trifle away to Katie to cheer her up, I realized I had only one left. Paul, tell me, how could I part with my only trifle?"

I looked Squire full in the face. In that moment, I saw not him, but Sarah. Immediately, I knew the truth. I had violated that little girl. I had marched into her world, uninvited and unannounced, to give her answers she did not need to questions she would never have needed to ask. I had imparted my wisdom and logic to her. But in her world, my wisdom and logic were nothing more than fool's folly. I had corrupted her. I had caused her to doubt. I had broken her spirit with distrust — distrust that had eventually broken the magic of the trifles. Quite simply, I had killed her. And through me, the whole town had been infected.

I was repulsed by the evil that I had brought upon Cromwell. I remembered how I had tried to warn Sarah of the evil that some men bring. I did not know at the time that I had been talking about myself. Turning from Squire, I went to the bathroom to throw up.

I stayed in Cromwell for a few more days, trying to right the wrong I had done. I talked to people, both individually and in groups, trying to convince them to cast away their fears and return to their old ways. I knew that if they did, then the magic of the trifles would return. Some listened. Most did not.

And so, I have left Cromwell, never to return. I do not know their fate. I do not know mine. Perhaps, in time, they will be able to purge themselves from my influence. Perhaps. And perhaps, in time, I will find a way to forgive myself for all the grief I have caused.

Another little Sarah with a pouch full of trifles is all it would take.

♠ ♠ ♠ ♠ ♠ ♠ ♠ ♠ ♠ ♠ ♠ ♠

Loyalty
By Little Johnny

♠ ♠ ♠ ♠ ♠ ♠ ♠ ♠ ♠ ♠ ♠ ♠

I knew something was wrong as soon as I came in the door that afternoon from school. Mom and Granny were sittin' on the couch in the living room, talkin' in hushed tones. Dad was leanin' in the doorway to the bedroom with a somber look on his face. As soon as Mom and Granny noticed I was home, they stopped talkin' and gave me a terrible woeful look.

"What's wrong, Mom?"

She looked at me and tried to speak, but she got choked up and started to sob. Granny followed suit. I still didn't know what was goin' on, but we all hugged-up and had a real good cry. For me, it was a strange, near-death experience. Granny was a big-bosomed woman, but Mom had practically nothing, if ya know what I mean. So there I was stuck between them, alternatin' between bein' nearly suffocated by Granny to bein' bumped and bruised by Mom's bony rib cage. After a couple of minutes, I managed to pull myself free.

"What's goin' on, Mom?" I repeated.

"It's your grandfather, Luther," she said. "We just came from the doctor and. . ." she started to choke-up again, "and. . ."

"Jitter!" came a gruff voice from the bedroom, "bring the boy in here, and I'll tell him myself."

The three of us went into Grandpa's room and gathered

96

around the bed. Dad remained in the doorway, silent. Grandpa was restin', all propped up with a pile of pillows. His face was ashen-white and his breathin' was labored. Granny Goldie took his hand and patted it gently.

Grandpa looked me straight in the eye and without hesitation declared, "I'm dyin', boy. Just got back from Doc Dailey, and he told me I had about a week to live. He told me there wasn't nothin' he could do, so he told me, in so many words, to go on home and die. So here I am."

Grandpa never was one to mince words, but for a ten-year-old, his announcement was mighty strong stuff. Oh, I knew Gramps had been ill for some time, but I always thought that it was a naggin' illness like Mom's headaches or Granny's corns. I'd never even considered that Grandpa was dyin'. We all had another good cry. This time I knew why.

Within a couple of days, the whole family had assembled. Back in those days, we didn't wait for a loved one to "pass away" to gather the family. Everybody wanted to be there in person to say their last good-byes. Uncle Jeep, Aunt Relda, Uncle Jack, Aunt Betty, Aunt Lucille, and Uncle Lawrence came in from Detroit. Uncle Harry and Aunt Aretta came from Cleveland, and Aunt Joann and Uncle Braden came from Tennessee. Counting all of the kids and favorite pets, at least thirty family members had descended upon Granny's little house to pay their last respects to the patriarch of the family.

Usually, family get-togethers were festive occasions. Uncle Jack, who made fishin' poles would always bring in a batch of new ones for all the boys. Uncle Harry always unloaded his latest collection of off-color jokes. He was also notorious for givin' head-rubs and jokin' with all the boys about their lack of hair on their chests. And Uncle Lawrence was always ready to take you for a ride in his

97

new convertible. Then there were Aunt Jo and Aunt Lucille, who had inherited a lot of physical attributes from Granny. They were always soft and fun to hug. But this gathering was full of somber recollections.

I remember sittin' at Granny's kitchen table late into the night, eatin' pecan pie and talkin' mostly about Grandpa. Funny, everybody talked as if he'd already passed on. Uncle Harry, Grandpa's oldest son, told us how Grandpa used to have a moonshine still back in the head of Coke Oven Hollow. He said that Grandpa used to be one of the biggest bootleggers on the creek. Opening up his shirt, he showed all us boys the forest of black hairs on his chest.

"This," he proclaimed, pointing to his chest, "is what a good diet of moonshine will do for ya."

Aunt Jo scolded him. She said he shouldn't be tellin' such yarns at a time like this. According to Jo, Grandpa was an honest, decent, hard-workin' coal miner who labored all day long for an indecent day's pay. The moonshine still was just something Harry had made up. Somehow, she didn't sound convincin'.

The next mornin' with the whole family there, we all filed into Grandpa's bedroom and hugged him one by one. And then we stood in silence, awaitin' Grampa's final words of wisdom to the family.

"Well, I guess y'all know why you're here, so there ain't much I got to tell ya." He paused to suck in air. "I guess I've lived a good life, and loved well and multiplied." We all looked around the room and chuckled. "I suppose I've had my share of lovin' and a decent share of good times. So before I go, I just want to tell y'all that I love ya, and don't worry about ol' Grandpa. Wherever he's goin', he'll be all right. Just promise me this: remember where ya came from, no matter where ya go."

Little Denise ran up and hugged him and we all joined

in, gathering closer to give Gramps, and ourselves, some encouragement.

"Now," he said, "y'all go get yourself some breakfast while someone helps me down to the courthouse."

"The courthouse?" asked Harry. "What are you gonna do? Change your will?"

"Pop," said Uncle Jack, "we can bring all that paper work here, if you want."

"Nope," insisted Grandpa, "I need to get down to the courthouse."

"For what, for goodness sakes?" asked Aunt Jo.

"To change my voter registration."

"To what?" everybody said in unison.

"To change my voter registration," repeated Grandpa with a cough.

"Why, Pop?" said Harry. "You've been a Democrat for fifty years. You're a union man who's hated Republicans all your life. What's the point in changin' now?"

"Because, son, if anybody's gonna die around here in this county, it's gonna be one of those no good scalawag Republicans!"

No one can ever say Grandpa didn't make the most of his life.

♠ ♠ ♠ ♠ ♠ ♠ ♠ ♠ ♠ ♠ ♠ ♠ ♠

The Visitation

♠ ♠ ♠ ♠ ♠ ♠ ♠ ♠ ♠ ♠ ♠ ♠ ♠

Jane Ann thought a whole army of people was descending upon her house. She came into the kitchen where Momma Pearl was getting ready to fix supper. She looked at Mamma Pearl's list: ham, mashed potatoes, green beans, corn, rolls, gravy, applesauce, cherry pie, beets, cucumbers, pickles, pea salad — the list went on and on. Jane Ann had no idea who or how many were coming, but for a feast like this, she knew they must be mighty important people. When she inquired who all the fixin's were for, Momma Pearl told her Aunt Peg was coming in from Kentucky for an extended visit.

"Just Aunt Peg?" she asked.

"What do you mean by *just Aunt Peg*, child. She's the only great-aunt you've got. I don't want to hear any of this *just* business."

"That's not what I mean, Momma Pearl. I knew Aunt Peg was coming, but it's just that Aunt Peg is only one person, and you're fixin enough for twenty."

"Well, we haven't seen her in two years. This calls for a celebration."

Jane Ann looked at all of the food being prepared. By the looks of it, not only had Aunt Peg not visited in two years, she hadn't eaten since then either. Momma Pearl continued to scurry around the kitchen, hastily making preparations.

100

"Tell you what, child. Your Pappa Bill's getting ready to head for the train station in Charleston to pick her up. Why don't you run along with him?"

The trip into town took over an hour. For Jane Ann, Charleston was always exciting. She lived in a little coal town of about three to four hundred people, but Charleston was a big city — forty, maybe fifty thousand people. The streets were always busy, and Charleston had more shops than anybody had money. When she and Pappa Bill arrived at the train station, it was bustling with activity, people coming and going in all directions.

The summer was hot, and the city was hotter still with all of its streets and buildings. The train station was filled with the rich smell of hot dogs floating out from the lunch counter. After a short wait, the billowing black smoke from the train could be seen in the distance. Then came several blasts of the whistle and the roar of the engines as the train settled into the station.

Aunt Peg was the first person to step from the train. She was a tall, thin woman in her early sixties. Her silver-white hair cascaded down around her shoulders like Christmas tensile. She was perhaps 5'8" or more and weighed no more than 110 pounds, but she was by no means frail. She walked with purposeful steps and carried herself with a regal air — quiet, dignified — a Kentucky thoroughbred. She spoke with a leisurely Kentucky drawl, a drawl that cannot be imitated, but only comes from years of exposure to bluegrass culture. She saw Jane Ann and Bill and smiled. Jane Ann ran to hug her.

"Well, my, my, Jane Ann, just look at you. You've grown so much. How old are you now? Thirteen?"

"Fourteen."

"And a mighty fine fourteen at that. And Bill, how you doin'? Staying away from trouble, I hope."

101

"Fine, Peg, just fine. You know, we weren't expectin'
you for another couple of weeks. Pearl's been rushin'
around all day in a tizzy, tryin' to get things ready before
you get there."

"Sister Pearl. When is she going to learn that I'm nobody special?"

The table was set when they arrived from the depot,
loaded down to be exact — and for good reason. Momma
Pearl had invited every cousin, niece, nephew, and stranger
to have supper with Aunt Peg. And, as it turned out, half
the town was related in one way or another. They all gathered around the table as Momma Pearl blessed the food,
and then everybody dug into the feast. It was a grand time,
thought Jane Ann — until she and her cousin Jeanie got
stuck cleaning up the dishes.

Over the next several days, Momma Pearl and Aunt Peg
spent their days filling each other in on all of the happen-
ings over the last two years. They went around visiting with
all the kinfolk and even took a shopping excursion into
Charleston. Jane Ann noticed that there was a continual air
of excitement wherever Aunt Peg went. For some reason,
she always provoked the best in those around her, even
from that scoundrel Uncle Manley. It was as if she possessed a secret energy, a secret charm, that attracted folks to
her. Jane Ann could not see why. She was just an old silver-
haired lady, no different from dozens of other silver-haired
ladies she knew. But for some reason, there was an aura
about her that other people lacked. Momma Pearl came
close to having it when she was preaching, but Peg seemed
to possess it all the time.

Later that week, Jane Ann and Peg found themselves
alone for the afternoon. Bill's sister, who lived at Ansted,
had taken ill, and he and Pearl decided to make a quick trip
over the mountain to visit her. Jane Ann and Aunt Peg were

left to fend for themselves for a day.

Jane Ann was accustomed to living with older people. Momma Pearl and Pappa Bill were not her mother and father. They were her grandparents, and she loved them dearly. Her mother had died during childbirth, and her father, for all intents and purposes, had abandoned her to be raised by Momma Pearl and Bill. Being an "only child" was no big problem, but the rejection and hatred from certain family members certainly were. It was almost too much for a young fourteen-year-old girl to handle.

Her father still lived in the area, but she rarely saw him. He came to visit perhaps twice a year. For sure, he would stop by at Christmas for about an hour to deliver a cheap present. But he never talked with her — only with Bill and Momma Pearl. They would sit in the living room. Her father would always sit in Pappa Bill's favorite armchair. She always resented that. With Jane Ann looking on, the three adults would chat for a while, but the uncomfortable conversations were never about important things. Occasionally, her father would ask her a question or two, but he was never genuinely interested in her answers. The whole gift-giving ritual was just a formality. There was definitely no love associated with the gifts. And she definitely did not consider him to be her father. (He was her sire, she would always tell folks.) And yet, his continual presence in the community was a constant reminder of his rejection of her and her unworthiness. When he remarried, and step-brothers and step-sisters came along, the rejection was only accentuated.

And then there was Uncle Manley, Momma Pearl's son. He was convinced that Jane Ann was going to steal his inheritance someday. It didn't matter that Pappa Bill was barely scraping by with a small grocery store and had very little to pass along. Uncle Manley, nonetheless, was obsessed with jealousy.

He was also possessed by a demon — alcohol to be exact. Jane Ann had witnessed many a drunken episode. Mostly, he fought with his wife, Corina, but sometimes he would come over to the house and threaten her — and Papa Bill — and Momma Pearl. It broke Momma Pearl's heart and made her cry and fall down on her knees in prayer. It would almost cause Pappa Bill to have a heart attack, leaving him reaching for his glycerin pills. And it frightened Jane Ann to her very core. Manley always carried a German luger, a handgun, that he had acquired during World War II. There were rumors that he had once killed a man — rumors he never denied.

And, so, she didn't mind the company of older folk like Aunt Peg. They were much more stable, loving, and accepting.

The afternoon with Aunt Peg was turning into a routine and somewhat boring event. It promised to be a day they both would soon forget. They fixed a simple meal and ate quietly. They talked very little. Perhaps Aunt Peg had talked herself out over the past week. Perhaps her boundless energy wasn't so boundless after all. Jane Ann started thinking about how boring the evening was going to be. Maybe, just maybe, Aunt Peg was great in a crowd, but wasn't so good one-on-one. Jane Ann was in for a revelation.

As the evening wore on, storm clouds began to gather on the horizon. Flashes of lightning could be see in the distance, and the thunder, faint at first, now grew more and more intense.

"Come on child. It's time for some evening entertainment." Aunt Peg led her to the porch, and they sat down on the porch swing.

"What are we going to do, Aunt Peg?"

"Watch the storm, Jane Ann, watch the storm."

Evening entertainment? Some evening entertainment, thought Jane Ann. She had seen lots of storms before. What was going to be entertaining and different about this one? Slowly, the storm clouds gathered, and the wind began to whip up the dust on the road beside the house. From their vantage point facing east, they could see the valley and the surrounding mountains as they became increasingly engulfed in the blackness being blown in from the west. A lightning bolt struck nearby.

"Can we go in, Aunt Peg?" Jane Ann was a bit frightened. She never did like lightning.

Aunt Peg surveyed the storm clouds and breathed in the air that was stirring all around. Her eyes brightened as if she sensed something — something that Jane Ann couldn't.

"I believe, child, if we're in the right spirit, we're in for a revelation tonight. So you pay close attention to this storm that's blowin' in. Think about where it came from and where it's going, who controls its path, and what revelations it may bring. Concentrate on all that's going on around you, child. Drink it all in. Drink it all in."

Aunt Peg trailed off to a whisper as the full force of the storm hit. They were in the midst of the storm now, but from the protection of the porch they could watch it safely, detached from all that was going on around them. The wind whipped around, and the rain blew by, occasionally spraying them with a mist. Leaves and paper swirled around in the air, being lifted up by the winds. The lightning flashed. The thunder rumbled. Before long, the whole valley was engulfed in the storm. The sky grew darker and darker until the whole valley was clothed in a wet, churning darkness, punctuated only by a massive lightning bolt every now and then.

Jane Ann sat with Aunt Peg, watching the storm and

wondering about her aunt's almost mystical preoccupation with it. This was certainly an impressive display of Mother Nature, but was there something else? Something she was missing?

The storm subsided and the rain slackened. The lightning receded up the valley. Night had settled in. Jane Ann conceded to herself that the storm had, indeed, been great entertainment.

"Aunt Peg, can we talk now? I'd really like to know about our picnic plans for tomorrow."

"Hush, child," Aunt Peg urged. "There's times for talkin' and there's times for keepin' silent. And this is one of those times for keepin' silent. Like I said before, if we're in the right spirit, we might just be witnesses to a revelation tonight. Something most folks have never seen and probably never will. But I've see it twice in my life, and it's always been on a night like this. . . Do you smell that smell?"

There was a faint, sweet odor in the air.

"What do you mean, Aunt Peg?" Jane Ann was beginning to think Aunt Peg was suffering from instant senility with all of this foolish talk.

"What I mean is this. We toil in the soil to earn our daily bread. We dig into the depths on the mountains to mine our coal. We labor at the lumber mill. But that's not why we were put on this earth, child. Oh, no. That's not the reason at all. All that working and toiling, all those trials and those troubles, they're just to prepare us for times like this. You see, we were really put here on this earth for moments like this, surrounded by the earth and its fullness, the night bathed in wonder and mystery, sitting in the midst of God's creation to commune with Him and His host of angels. That's why we were put here. Do you know what I'm saying, child?"

"Well, no, not really, Aunt Peg."

"Well, just be still, honey — in your body, soul, and spirit," Aunt Peg's voice dropped to a whisper, "and I'll show you the angels tonight. I can smell them a-comin'."

"The what?"

"The angels, child. God's angels. Now, if you want to see them, you have to keep real still, settle down inside yourself, and open your spiritual eyes."

This talk of angels sent a shiver down Jane Ann's spine. Aunt Peg was earnest and dead-serious. In the light of day, she would have considered such talk about seeing angels as something foolish — daffy. But in the still of this night, with the lightning flashing on the distant mountain peaks, the thought of seeing angels was altogether believable. And Aunt Peg's earnest, serious tone convinced her all the more that something spectacular was about to happen.

"How do we do it, Aunt Peg? See the angels, I mean."

"Just hush-up and let the night take you in. Feel it all around you. Let it fill your mind, and then open your heart and spirit to the possibilities. Some folks say 'seeing is believing', but I say believing is seeing."

Aunt Peg's talk was more than a bit unnerving. Jane Ann had never heard her talk like this before. But now, more than ever, she was beginning to believe her crazy talk. And there *was* a peculiar odor in the air.

They settled into silence again. Following Aunt Peg's instructions, Jane Ann closed her eyes to concentrate. At first, her ears were filled with the normal sounds of a post-storm night. Water dripping from the roof, from the trees, running through the gullies, rivers rising with new life-blood, an occasional breeze through the leaves, crickets, frogs, the wisp of a light rising fog brushing her face, the sound of a bat swooping past the tree tops, an occasional distant rumble from the dying storm, people talking in the night, porches creaking, puddles splashing, spiders weaving, possums scampering, flowers stretching, leaves reaching, trees yawning, valleys whispering, mountains breathing.

Suddenly there was a rush of a new presence in the air. Perhaps it had been there all the time, and she was just now becoming aware of it. Perhaps Aunt Peg had felt it all along. She looked over at Aunt Peg and sensed that she felt it, too. A smile was on her aunt's face, and her eyes, gleaming in the darkness, grew wide open, taking in everything before her.

"What is that?" said Jane Ann, somehow knowing that Aunt Peg would know what she was talking about.

"The angels," whispered Aunt Peg. "Now hush. They're about to descend!"

A sudden gust of wind encircled the house. It came up from behind, rushing around the corners and continued up the valley in the direction of the retreating storm. The trees bent over, the house creaked, and all around there were objects in the air — thousands and thousands of objects — faint moon-glow objects, large and small, rushing to and fro amongst the houses. They swarmed over the porch where she and Aunt Peg were, crowding in around where they sat. With them came an electric-like charge, filling the air along with an intensified sweet, strangely familiar odor. Quickly, these flickering moon-glows wove through the trees, brushing aside the branches. They filled the valley and mountainsides with specks of light as they dashed and darted through the air. Like a giant army in a mighty swarm, they proceeded swiftly upon the wind, racing up the valley floor, and disappeared into the thundercloud in the distance. They left as suddenly as they had appeared.

Aunt Peg raised both arms into the air, palms open and facing forward. "Yes! Yes! Praise the Lord, child, did you see them? Did you see them?"

Jane Ann was stunned. It had all happened so quickly. They were here, and then they were there, and then they were gone. She could not understand what she had just seen. It was too glorious to take in.

"Yes, Aunt Peg, yes. What was that?"

"The angels, my child, the angels. God's holy angels."

Jane Ann had read about angels in the Bible, but they had never been real to her. They had just been part of the story. Gabriel. Michael. The heavenly hosts. Sure she believed in them, but they had never been *real* to her before. She began to cry and hyperventilate with excitement.

"The angels, Aunt Peg? You mean *the* angels?"

"Yes, child, yes. *The* angels. You see, I told you we weren't put here just to work and eat and drink and sleep and fight with Uncle Manley. *This* is why we were made. This is why we are here — to glory in and glorify all of God and His creation. Even the angels."

"Will they come back?" Jane Ann asked breathlessly.

"Ah, child, that's the beauty of it. They have not left. They were here all the time. Still are. We're just not privileged to always see them. But they're here all right. And so is the Lord God Jehovah. Don't you ever forget that. So when you're hurtin', child, or when you're sad — when that rascal Manley gives you a hard time — when you think you don't have a soul in the world who cares for you — just remember you always have someone in heaven who cares for you, and He's got His angels right here with you all the time. Do you believe that, child?"

"I do now, Aunt Peg. I surely do now."

"Good. Now live like you believe it."

"Will we see them again?"

"Maybe. Maybe not. Some folks never see them, so count yourself blessed. And you may never see them again in this life. But let me tell you something, honey. It's not the seeing, it's the believing — it's the knowing that's important. It's the knowing. That, child, is what will always bless both you and those around you."

They lapsed into silence. The air was still filled with the smell of angels, and Jane Ann wondered how she could ever tell anyone what she had seen that night. After much contemplation, she decided to keep it a secret — her and Aunt Peg's secret. Besides, no one, especially at school, would believe her. She thought forward to the years ahead with assurance. Perhaps someday when she had children, she would be able to share Peg's secret — her secret — with them.

And even if she never saw the angels again, she would always enjoy the presence of their company and the lingering sweet, sweet smell they leave behind after a summer's rain.

♠ ♠ ♠ ♠ ♠ ♠ ♠ ♠ ♠

Small Seeds

♠ ♠ ♠ ♠ ♠ ♠ ♠ ♠ ♠

There were no promises to keep today. No appointments. No deadlines. Only some smooth, sun-brewed tea and a folding chair under an evening shade tree. The humid breeze. The fragrance of summer. Thousands of bugs in the air. One-of-a-kind bugs, never seen before. Never to be seen again. A waning sun over the crest of the ridge. Growing shadows. A familiar peace welling up from the "hollers" and mountains.

I had often wondered why I had stayed here — in the hills — away from the *real* world with all of its busyness. Promises full of life. Purposeful. Meaningful. Occupied with accomplishments and challenges. I'd been chided by some for my failure — to step out — to seek my fortune — to make my mark. What kind of life could you possibly have here on "the creek?" No opportunities. No entertainment. No new horizons. A waste of talent, I had been told. *The eyes of man are never satisfied.*

I had often questioned myself for not being more ambitious, more outgoing, more — more of whatever you're suppose to be — out there — in the real world. But somehow, on evenings like this, I knew all about the real world. And it did not lie "out there." On evenings like this, I wondered about the validity of other people's realities.

A car stopped by the house. A strange car. A woman, unfamiliar, emerged from the driver's side.

111

"Bradley? Bradley Thompson? Is that you?"

It was Elizabeth Williams. Lizzy. I hadn't seen Lizzy Williams in ten — no make that fifteen years — at least. She ran up to hug me. Planted a wet kiss on my cheek.

"Bradley Thompson, you rascal, you don't look a day over thirty-five."

"And you don't look a day over fifty-two."

I was joking. Sort of. Both of us were about the same age: forty-three, forty-four. After a while, you lose count. And she didn't look a day over fifty-two. Fifty maybe, but not fifty-two. Graying hair. Rounding belly. Wrinkles around the eyes. Smoker's wrinkles.

"Still smoking are you? Never could get you to stop, could I?"

"Well, what a way to greet a friend. Seventeen years and it takes you ten seconds to start naggin'."

Seventeen years. So it had been seventeen years. We were young, then.

"Pull up a chair. Make yourself comfortable."

"I stopped, you know."

"Stopped what?"

"Smoking, Bradley, smoking."

She had lost her mountain accent. I swear, she sounded like a born-again Yankee. She kinda looked like one too, dressed in her expensive business outfit.

"Yeah? How long?"

Lizzy looked at her watch.

"Oh, fifteen, twenty minutes." She reached for her purse. "Got a match?" Old joke. We both laughed anyway.

"Well, Lizzy Williams, what brings you here? How's Carl?"

"Divorced."

"Divorced?"

"Don't want to talk about him, Bradley. Besides, I came

112

to see you, to share some memories — I even brought you a present."

"What are you up to, Lizzy? Did you come a-courtin'?"

"You'll see, but let's talk first."

And so we did. Small talk at first. About family. About friends. Joyce was living in LA, doing unspecified films. Got burned out by the wild fires last fall. Aaron was practicing law for some big corporation. Weighed three hundred pounds, at least. Sharon had died in an auto accident, and Martin was teaching at the university. And Carl, her high-school sweetheart?

"Carl doesn't exist. We're divorced. Physically and legally separated." That's all she would say.

"OK. But what about you, Lizzy? What about you?"

Still working for Senator Ralston. Wheelin'. Dealin'. Deadlines. Press conferences. Important meetings. Blah-de-blah-de-blah-de-blah.

"Bradley, did you know that journalists are the butts of the world?"

"No, really?"

"Yeah." She impersonates an eyewitness-anchorperson. "Senator Ralston is leading in the polls — *but*. Senator Ralston's speech was well received — *but*. The weather is perfect tonight — *but*. You get the picture?"

"Yeah, I see what you mean, *but* that's not why you came here, is it, Lizzy?"

"No. I came to reminisce a bit — and I brought you a present." She paused. "Do you remember our mission trip to Charlotte?"

Our mission trip to Charlotte? My mind had completely forgotten about that summer. Forgotten until Lizzy reminded me, and then, in a split second, my brain conjured up in random fashion a collage of events. Memories flashed into my consciousness, and were quickly assembled into

113

sequence. Yes, yes, the mission trip. It was the summer before our senior year in high school. We had been enlisted to help a struggling church in the ghettos of Charlotte with Vacation Bible School. Calvin, our youth director, had been so convincing about how important it was for us to "serve the Lord."

I remembered arriving in Charlotte after a long bus trip and unloading our gear. We stayed at a nearby college dorm. We were warned not to bring any valuables. "They'll steal you blind." "Better lock your doors." But Carl and I ignored the warnings. By the following night, he had lost a baseball glove, and my transistor radio was missing. And we had come to help. We had come to "serve the Lord."

The following morning — where was I? Yes, the following morning, I was in the basement of the church. I was fixing Kool Aid. I had come 250 miles to fix Kool Aid and get my radio swiped. Those were my thoughts at the time. Was this what Calvin meant by changing the world? I didn't think so. But when the kids came downstairs, suddenly everything changed. They were black kids. Many of them were wearing well-worn clothes. Clothes that didn't fit — ironically, clothes that we had brought with us from the poverty-filled hills of West Virginia. But the kids were so excited. They were so eager to sing the songs and play the games and drink my Kool Aid. The pastor explained to us the poverty in which they lived. When I understood that, I almost didn't blame the one who had stolen my stuff. I said almost. That night, we locked our dorm rooms.

The next day we went hunting for my radio and Carl's glove. We found my radio with a young kid, maybe ten years old, sitting on a porch step. Calvin went up the steps. Carl and I stayed behind on the sidewalk.

"Give ya three dollars for it," Calvin offered.

"OK," the kid said, handing Calvin the radio.

114

"My friend back there has the money," said Calvin. "I'll be right back."

Calvin came down the steps and, when he got to Carl and me, whispered "Run!" We ran as fast as we could and never looked back for fear of who might have been chasing us.

Calvin. Calvin, my Christian youth director, had lied. Sure he got my radio back, but he had lied. I chuckled at the memory.

The next day found me back in the basement making Kool Aid when this young kid came running into the kitchen area. He was clutching his stomach. It was the same young kid who had stolen my radio! At first, I thought he was hurt. But the pants. I noticed the pants. The pants were way too big. They were castoff pants from my neighborhood, but they were all he had. And he had no belt. That was why he was clutching his stomach. At recess, I saw him trying to play, holding his pants up with one hand and catching and throwing the ball with the other. That's when I gave him my belt. Thief or no thief, he deserved a belt. Thief or no thief, he deserved a little dignity. It was the least I could do.

That night Carl's glove had been returned to the dorm.

I remembered how at the end of the week none of the kids wanted us to leave. We didn't either. I remembered smiling faces, craving love and acceptance. I remembered feeling guilty leaving them behind.

"Bradley," said Lizzy, interrupting my remembering, "do you remember our trip to Charlotte?"

"Yes, Lizzy, I do. . . We thought we could change the world back then, didn't we?"

"That's just it, Bradley. We did change the world. At least, you did."

"What do you mean?"

115

"Here." She handed me a small box. "I have a present for you. Open it."

I unwrapped the box and opened it to find my old belt — the old belt I had given away twenty-five years ago. I could still see my initials carved on the inside.

"I don't understand," I said. "I gave this away twenty-five years ago."

"It's from Jerome Watson."

"*The* Jerome Watson? The head of the African Relief effort?"

"Yes. *The* Jerome Watson, who tirelessly reaches out across the globe to help people in need. There's no finer man in the world."

"But?"

"I met him in New York last week. He was meeting with Senator Ralston just before he went back to Africa to oversee the relief effort. After the meeting, in the midst of some small talk, we came to discover that we had met many years ago. In a ghetto. In Charlotte. Bradley, Jerome is the little kid who stole your radio. He's the little kid that you gave your belt to."

"But — "

"Jerome said you changed his life that day. Your generosity, but much more important, your forgiveness changed his life. He says you make the best Kool Aid in the world, too."

I found myself chuckling.

"But it was such a small thing," I mused.

"Sometimes small things are all it takes to make us, or to break us, to lift us up, or to let us down. And that day, when you gave away your belt, you lifted a little kid out of poverty. Not physically, but spiritually. Oh, it wasn't easy, but Jerome vowed that day to change his life and not be trapped by his circumstances. And he kept your belt as a reminder. In fact, as crazy as this sounds, whenever he had something really important to do, he would carry your belt in his brief case. But last week, when he discovered that I knew you and where you lived, he insisted I return this to you. With his deepest thanks, of course."

Small seeds silently sown oft times sprout and flourish beyond our expectations.

I leaned back in my lawn chair and smiled. It was a perfect evening on the creek.

♠ ♠ ♠ ♠ ♠ ♠ ♠ ♠ ♠ ♠ ♠ ♠

Movie Magic
By Little Johnny

♠ ♠ ♠ ♠ ♠ ♠ ♠ ♠ ♠ ♠ ♠ ♠

One good thing about livin' on Loop Creek is gettin' off of it for a change. Now that might sound like double talk, but it ain't. Sometimes you get tired of all the country and simply have to get into a big city like Oak Hill for a change. With 5,000 people, Oak Hill has a lot more to offer than the creek. For example, they have a department store with three colors of pants to choose from, and a dairy mart where you can get a 39-cent banana split. And then there's Tom's Carry Out for footlong hot dogs and the drug store where you can buy a double-cherry Coke float. But I suppose the one thing that the big city has to offer that the country doesn't is the drive-in movie theater. And Oak Hill has two of them, one on each end of town!

The best part about goin' to the drive-in is all of the ritual surroundin' it. First, you have to decide if you're goin' or not. That's not an easy task. No, sir. About five in the afternoon, the questions begin. Think we should go to the drive-in? Who's goin'? Uncle Jeep, you want to take us tonight? Karen's not goin', is she? That's when everybody starts jockeyin' for position. That's because there's too much family and too little car. Oh, sometimes Dad will break down and take his car, too, but not often, so don't count on it. Most families fight about land, or money, or serious things like that. But at our place, there's been many a family "discussion" about just who was goin' and who was bein' left behind on Friday night. It's about the only thing I know my family actually fights about.

One major decision maker is the weather. It seems every time we decide to go, the sky begins to cloud up to rain. And so, you're always on edge, wondering if Mother Nature is gonna cooperate. The anticipation is as excitin' as a tug on your trout line. Is it gonna rain? Will it be too foggy? Serious questions with monumental consequences.

Now, I don't know about your family's decision-makin' methods, but the last thing that we consider at our house is the movie that's playing. Over the years, we've seen some classics: *The Sound and the Fury* (a werewolf story), *Gone with the Wind* (a vampire story), and *The Grapes of Wrath*. (A bunch of giant, radioactive grapes destroy a small town in New Mexico.) But the best one was *The Black Widow Spiders* — an artsy, foreign film where all the women pranced around in black underwear. Uncle Jeep brought us home early that night. So, you see, we don't pay much attention to the titles. Generally, we end up goin' to the drive-in that has the family-night discount for that week.

The grand finale of the gettin'-ready-for-the-drive-in ritual is the poppin' of the corn. There's no way that a high-class poor family like us is gonna pay 25 cents for a box of popcorn. Besides, Mom makes the best popcorn on the creek. Once the decision is made to go, Mom will haul out the three-gallon green bean pot and the five-gallon can of "Pure Lard", and the popcorn poppin' begins! Sometimes Mom will pop two grocery bags full, enough to last through a doubleheader and still have some for the next day. Mom's especially proud of her poppin' skills and will always give folks instructions as she goes along.

"First," she says, "you've got to make sure that the pot

is larded-up real good. There's nothing worse than dry pop-corn." She scoops out a big soup spoon full of white stuff and drops it into the pot. "Remember, never put the corn into a cold pot. The grease has got to be simmerin' hot first." She waits patiently for the grease to start cracklin', and then she pours the corn to it. Within no time, the corn is poppin', and Mom is shakin the pot like crazy. It's like an assembly line. The pot fills up, and she dumps it in the grocery bag, and it fills up some more, and she dumps some more, and with every dump, she furiously throws the salt to it. "The secret is to salt it while it's hot," she says. "If you wait two seconds too long, the corn will cool off, and the salt won't stick to it. You'll wind up with tasteless corn and all the salt in the bottom of the bag."

Sometimes, when Mom really gets into the poppin' mood, we'll have enough to last all the way into Monday — if you like cold, greasy, salty popcorn.

After the popcorn poppin', we all load up in the car and head for the drive-in. You can tell the men from the boys (and the girls from the women) by their pillows. Some peo-ple plan on doin' more sleepin' than movie watchin'. I al-ways wondered why they went to the movies in the first place, if they were gonna fall asleep in the middle of *The Agony and the Ecstasy* (another vampire movie).

When we arrive at the drive-in, all us kids usually head for the playground. It seems like the drive-in has got the biggest, fastest swing set in the world. And so, we swing away, anxiously awaitin' for the sun to go down and the sky to get dark.

I always linger a bit longer at the playground, even after the other kids head for the car. You see, at my age, there's always the possibility that that strange, magical girl of my dreams will happen by and invite me to her car to watch the movie. So far, I'm still awaitin' for her to show up.

Finally, the sky grows dark, and the projector starts up, and the Smithfield Bar-B-Q commercials (Ya-hoo!) flash on the screen, and the smell of hot dogs and French fries — and popcorn — pour out of the concession stand. Show time is here! It's now time for the main attraction — human blood for hungry mosquitoes.

Actually, the idea of a drive-in movie is much better than the reality of a drive-in movie. The air is always muggy. The car is always stuffy. Someone's always too hot. If you roll the windows down, the bugs swarm in, bitin' ya half to death. If you roll the windows up, the windshield fogs up. There's not enough room in the back seat for four kids and three pillows. Fights break out. The speaker doesn't work. It starts rainin'. The movie projector goes on the blink. Brother Tom spills his drink on his pillow. Sister Karen spills half the popcorn in the floor. (And sometimes she puts it back in the bag without tellin' ya about it.) And at the end of the evenin', Uncle Jeep vows to never again take us to the drive-in. All in all, I'd say it's quite an enjoyable adventure.

But the best part, aside from the popcorn (now mixed with floor-grit), is the ride home. The night is dark, and the rain is pourin' down, or the fog is thickenin' up as the headlights from the car snake through the mountain night. The trees and bushes press in beside the road. As the lights flash around the curve, you can catch a glimpse of that vampire or werewolf you saw at the drive-in, lurkin' in the trees. Indeed, there is mystery in the midnight mountain air. You just know that ghoul will be in your bedroom or right outside your window, waiting for you when you get home. Some folks call that the magic of movies. It's something you'll find only in the big cities like Oak Hill.

♠ ♠ ♠ ♠ ♠ ♠ ♠ ♠ ♠ ♠ ♠ ♠ ♠ ♠ ♠ ♠ ♠ ♠ ♠ ♠

The Last Second Chance

♠ ♠ ♠ ♠ ♠ ♠ ♠ ♠ ♠ ♠ ♠ ♠ ♠ ♠ ♠ ♠ ♠ ♠ ♠ ♠

Cigar smoke filled the room, a honky-tonk song blared out on the jukebox, and the wooden floor creaked under foot as Manley, with one elbow resting on the counter, downed another beer. Still, it didn't help. The anger and frustration were still there. He hadn't planned to come to the Coal Dust Cavern tonight. He hadn't planned to drink too much. In fact, he was never one to plan much of anything. Just let it flow was his philosophy. If you felt like workin', work. If you felt like fightin', fight. If you felt like drinkin', drink. And tonight, more than any other, he felt like drinkin'. So he drank.

There was a deep, slow burning rage inside him — a rage that he could neither define nor understand. But more important, it was a rage he was unable to squelch. His life, it seemed, had always been thwarted by restrictions. *What right does Corina have to tell me what to do? She's only a woman — there to keep the house and tend to the kids and keep me company when I want company. But what right does she have to tell me what to do with my time? And what right does she have to tell me what to do with my money? After all, it's my money — not hers — not the kids. I work hard for that money; risk my life for it, and I have every right to spend it as I well please — both my time and my money.*

122

The drinking helped — a little. It helped the pain, but it didn't erase the hate. He remembered that day down by the river when he had gotten into a fight with his younger sister. He remembered being drunk and slapping her. *I musta been skunk drunk to have done that. Skunk drunk.* He fought his emotions that were churning inside him and took another drink. Yes, that was the day Gene, his sister's boyfriend, had beaten him up — beaten him up rather soundly, as a matter of fact. He still had a deep bruise under one eye that had not completely healed. Ordinarily, he would have shot Gene over that — killed him. He wondered now why he hadn't. After all, killing a man didn't mean much. He had done it before and had even been rewarded for doing so.

"I served in Europe during the war," he said, thinking out loud about his bravery, talking to no one in particular. The two men beside him ignored him as he rambled on. "Saw many a man killed. Killed several myself." He leaned toward Tommy Lee beside him, reached in his back pocket, and pulled out a pearl-handled gun. "That's where I got this. Killed a man with my bare hands for it, Tommy Lee. Ya hear me? Killed him with my bare hands."

Tommy Lee's eyes opened wide, and he began to pay very close attention to Manley's story, not because it was interesting, but because Manley was recklessly waving the handgun in the air.

"Manley, is that gun loaded?"

Manley was too wrapped up in himself and too loaded with booze to pay any attention to anyone else, much less Tommy Lee.

"Run him through with a bayonet like this." Manley took the gun and plunged it into Tommy Lee's stomach. "And then I twisted it like this," he said, giving the gun a half turn into Tommy Lee's gut.

123

By this time, Tommy Lee had quickly sobered up and was paying the utmost attention to Manley's story. He sat motionless, afraid to say anything. He had heard of men having flashbacks, thinking they were back on the battlefield, jumping at cars, grabbing things and wrestling them to the ground. And he didn't want to do anything that would cause Manley to think that he was a German Nazi soldier.

Manley looked Tommy Lee straight in the eyes. The barrel of the gun was firmly pressed into his stomach. Manley stared at him, and Tommy Lee stared hopelessly back. Manley's eyes formed a cold, drunken, unblinking stare — the kind of stare that made an atheist like Tommy Lee into an instant believer. Tommy Lee bit his lip and a plaintiff sigh escaped from his mouth. The whole bar, finally realizing what was happening, became hushed. Someone unplugged the jukebox, and Hank William's twangy voice wound down into silence.

"And then I stared him in the eyes and watched him squirm and die." Tommy Lee tried his best not to squirm. "And then I pried this gun out of his bloody, little, dead hand." Manley pulled the gun from Tommy Lee's gut and placed it on the counter. "Wanna see it? Look, there on the handle, just like I said, a German swastika."

Tommy Lee quickly picked up the gun for safekeeping as Manley turned back within himself with his thoughts. He staggered over to a table and sat down, caring not that he had abandoned his prized gun. *Yes, I coulda shot Gene for beatin' me up. I can still do it. That's it. I'll kill the little weasel anyway. Yep, I'll drive right over there tonight and shoot him through the head. I'll just walk up to his house, and when he opens the door — Bam! — I'll pull out my gun like this and . . .* Manley reached into his back pocket for his gun and discovered that it was missing.

I could swear I had my gun. Where's my gun?

Just then Tommy Lee turned at the bar and raised Manley's gun into the air for inspection.

"Hey! Tommy Lee! Whataya doin' with my gun?"

"You gave it to me, Manley."

"I did no such thing. Now, why are you tryin' to steal my gun?"

"I ain't, Manley. Honest. You pulled it outa your back pocket and stuck it in my gut. Don't ya remember? You coulda killed me."

"I will kill ya, you little skunk, if ya steal my gun."

Manley picked up a chair and started toward Tommy Lee. Surprised by Manley's attack, Tommy Lee dropped the gun on the floor and began to back away. Suddenly, the lights went out, and that was the last thing Manley remembered of that night at the Coal Dust Cavern.

The next morning, he awoke to the blast of a towboat whistle. Startled and scrambling to sit up, he hit his head on the steering wheel of his car. Alternating between rubbing his head and rubbing his eyes, he slowly realized where he was — down on the river bank in his car. Looking around, he discovered Tommy Lee, who was sleeping in the back seat. As he leaned back, he sat on something uncomfortable. It was his prized German handgun. *Well, at least I got my gun back without killin' Tommy Lee.* The towboat whistle blasted again, and Tommy Lee began to stir. As he did, he stirred up a putrid smell that filled the car. Last night he had puked all over the back seat.

As Manley reacted to the stench, a gentle mist rolled across the river. Manley wondered what day it was. He wondered how he and Tommy Lee had managed to become friends again. He wondered how they had made it down here to the river. He wondered if Corina would let him back into his house this morning.

He dropped Tommy Lee off at the company store where

he did some recuperating before heading home. He knew Corina would be upset. When he pulled up to the backyard of his house, Corina was outside, hanging laundry to dry. He opened the gate and tried walking through the yard as if nothing had happened.

"Morning, Corina," he said in the most normal voice he could muster.

Corina said nothing, but gave him a cold stare that put a chill in the spring air around them.

"You were supposed to take Teddy fishin' this mornin', Manley."

"I'll catch him later, Corina. Right now my head's splittin' in two."

"Don't come crying to me, Manley Price. You got what you paid for. Now, get outta my sight before I strangle ya with this clothes line."

Ordinarily, those were fighting words, but this morning Manley's head hurt too badly for fighting. His whole body hurt too badly for fighting. He retreated into the backdoor and then stopped.

"Oh, yes," he said, waving his hand toward the car, "you and Teddy clean that thing up. Tommy Lee puked all over it last night." It mattered not that Teddy was only five years old. With that he entered the house, went into his bedroom, and collapsed on the bed.

Later that afternoon, Manley rolled over in his bed. The sun fell directly on his face. He squinted and sat up as his brain started to function again. He looked at his watch. *Geez. I gotta be at work in two hours.* His mouth was dry, and his body ached all over. He was in no condition to go to work, and he certainly didn't want to stay home and fight with Corina. *Better git on out of the house before Corina finds out that I'm up.* It was easier that way — being out of the house — easier for him and easier for Corina. By now,

126

the liquor had worn off completely, and he was dreadfully hungry. But he knew Corina would be in no mood to cooperate. So, he decided to drop in and see his mom. Perhaps he could mooch a good meal from her. Quietly, he slipped on his shoes and slipped out the back door to his car. When he got inside, the odor nearly took his breath away. *I'm gonna kill that stinkin', pukin', whinin' Tommy Lee.* Corina had not cleaned the car. In fact, unknown to Manley, she had added a load of table scraps to the mix, instead.

"Hi, Momma Pearl. It's me Manley," he called as he entered his mother's front door.

"Back here, Manley. In the kitchen."

He found Pearl getting ready to feed a baby. The sink was full of dishes, and there was no food on the stove except for some milk warming in a bottle. He was tempted to drink it.

"When are ya gettin' rid of the little leech, Ma?" he said as he rummaged through her refrigerator. "You know yer gettin' too old to take care of a little one like that. Jeanie oughta be doing that."

"Just look at her, Manley. Ain't she beautiful?"

Manley looked down at the red, wrinkled mass of flesh.

"Looks like an oversized, bleached-out prune to me."

He never could understand how women could call babies beautiful. They cried. They screamed. They soiled their own clothes and slept in it. They stunk. They wanted their way or no way. They cried out for constant attention. Kind of like Tommy Lee. A lot like Tommy Lee.

"Manley Price! I'll have none of that talk in my house. Now, this is your sister Jeanie's baby. Your niece. And she's the prettiest baby on Loop Creek, perhaps the whole state of West Virginia. And she's not a leech. She's a helpless baby. Here, hold her a bit and love her."

She offered him the baby, and with Momma Pearl doing

127

the offering, it was one thing he found hard to refuse. So, he found himself standing there in the middle of the kitchen with the baby in his arms, feeling extremely awkward. He wasn't comfortable with babies — not even his own. He didn't quite know how to handle them. And so he stood there holding her with his stomach screaming for food. He wished he could be somewhere else.

Momma Pearl looked at her son. He wasn't such a bad boy, she told herself. Mothers have a knack for seeing the best in their children. If he could just stay away from that liquor, he might make something of himself. Concern for her son was perhaps the one great thorn in her side, a cross that she bravely bore. For years, she had prayed for him. Daily, she had prayed for him, but his drinking only seemed to get worse. Why is it, she often wondered, why is it that she could preach such thrilling sermons? Why is it that God could use her to save and bless others and, yet, she could not save her own son? The baby cooed and smiled. Manley involuntarily smiled back.

"See. Look at that, Manley, she likes you."

"Mom, can you fix me something to eat? I've been workin' all day, and Corina is off down the road with Teddy somewhere."

"Sure, Manley, sure. Come sit down."

"And can I put this baby down?"

"Not until I've fixed you something to eat. Now you just sit down here and feed this bottle to the baby, and I'll fry you up a couple of hamburgers. And don't forget to burp her."

What a man won't do for a little food. It was at times like these he wished he was down at the Coal Dust Cavern with Tommy Lee. Old Tommy Lee might stink, and cry, and soil his clothes, but at least he could burp himself.

Earl Craddock was nuzzling up to his second beer when

Manley got to the Coal Dust Cavern. Pearl's two hamburgers had renewed Manley's energy, and his thirst. Just a couple before going to work would do. Besides Earl, there were only a couple of other people in the bar. It was the usual crowd for a mid-afternoon on a week day, and Manley was barely noticed when he entered. Andy, the bartender, greeted him and served up his usual drink.

Manley sat in silence, drinking his beer and wondering how he could avoid going to work and still get paid. *A creative mind should be able to come up with a creative solution.* While he was deep in thought, the door to the tavern swung open and a woman entered. She walked without hesitation and sat down on the stool beside Manley.

"Hello, Manley," she said.

"Do I know you?" asked Manley, squinting his eyes.

He was sure he had never see this woman before, and he certainly wasn't accustomed to a such forward, friendly female, especially at the Coal Dust. Manley concentrated on her face. She wore her hair short and had a young-mature look that made him wonder just how old she really was. *She ain't particularly pretty, but she's certainly interesting to look at.* Manley was still trying to decide if she was twenty-five or forty-five when she spoke again.

"Yes and no," she said. "My name is Myra."

"Myra?" Manley thought out loud, attempting to place the face and name. "I don't know no Myra."

"Manley, who are you takin' to?" asked Andy.

Myra motioned toward Andy and said rather nonchalantly, "He can't see me, Manley. And he can't hear me, either. Only you can do that."

"What?" said Manley. "Whataya mean he can't see you? Yer sittin' right here in front of me."

Andy picked up Manley's bottle and inspected it. "Have you been drinkin' before you got here, Manley? Is that why

129

you're talkin' to yourself?"

"No," said Manley, "I'm sittin' here talkin' to Myra."

"I told you he can't see me," warned Myra.

"What in the blazes are you talkin' about, Manley? There ain't nobody here 'cept Earl and Clem and ol' Jessup sittin back there in the corner."

"He really can't see you!" said Manley, looking and talking directly to Myra. She was sitting no more than three feet from where Andy was standing.

"Of course, I can't see her," said Andy, clearly agitated. "In fact, I don't even know who you're talkin' to — or about — or whatever."

"I suggest we go outside to continue this conversation, Manley," said Myra calmly. "That way Andy won't have you arrested again."

Bewildered, Manley stared at Myra's smiling face for some time, thinking that he might be hallucinating. Finally, he said, "OK, then, let's go outside."

"You're crazy, Manley. As long as I got customers, I ain't leavin' from behind this counter."

"No, not you, Andy. Myra. Myra and me are goin' outside ta talk."

Manley plunked down a dollar, told Andy to keep the change, and followed Myra out to the parking lot. As they left, Earl and Andy could only look at each other and shrug their shoulders in bewilderment.

"I told ya he couldn't hold his liquor," said Earl.

Outside, Myra motioned toward her automobile. "Want to sit in my car?" she said. "I think we'll have some privacy there."

Manley pulled up his collar against a cold wind that was now blowing, and got in on the passenger's side. As Myra got in and closed the door, Manley stared at her curiously. She seemed familiar to him now, but he still could not place her.

"Are you a ghost? Is that why Andy couldn't see you?"

"Oh, no," said Myra, "you don't ever want to meet a real ghost. They are much more frightening and dangerous than I will ever be."

"Then what are you? A bad bottle a booze?"

"I'm your guardian angel, Manley, and I've come to give you your last second chance."

"You're my what?"

"Your guardian angel, Manley, and I've come to —"

"I heard ya. Give me a second chance." He rubbed his face, stared at Myra, and smiled. "So, yer my guardian angel. Well, prove it."

"Remember when you were eight, and you fell through the ice in the river, and there was no one around to pull you out?"

"Yep."

"I was the one who came along and rescued you."

Manley stared intently at her face. Of course! That's where he had seen her before. She had come out of nowhere that day and pulled him from the icy waters. And she had just as quickly disappeared. She had not changed in almost twenty years. *I must be dreamin'*.

"Well, I don't think I'm drunk, but this certainly is the derndest hallucination I've ever had," said Manley, rubbing his throat and trying to make sense out of the turn of events. "Is this like Scrooge where there's three of ya that come along, and show me my past, present, and future, and try and git me ta git in the givin' spirit, and give all my money away? 'Cause if it is, yer a little too late. This is April."

"No, Manley. This is serious. I have come to warn you and give you your last second chance."

Manley smirked. "Then are ya gonna whisk me away in the spirit and show me all the wrong things I done in the

131

past? 'Cause if ya are, it ain't gonna do ya no good. I know I've been a hell-raiser — drinkin' and carousin'. And I wanna tell ya, it don't bother me none, either."

"So you don't want to see your past, do you, Manley? Come on, I'll show you your past anyway. And it isn't pretty."

She pulled from the parking lot at the Coal Dust Cavern and drove along the road. The sky was becoming increasingly overcast with the threat of rain. As they drove along, Manley finished the beer that he had brought with him from the tavern and started humming a country tune. Suddenly, the humming stopped.

"Wait a minute. Where are we goin'?" Manley asked, as Myra turned onto an unfamiliar road. That was not possible. He knew every nook and hollow along Loop Creek. But where they were going, he had never been before. After a few minutes, the car pulled through a set of ornamental iron gates. The field in front of them was strewn with graves and headstones.

"Where are we at?" asked Manley.

"We're in your past," said Myra. "All of these monuments are your handy work."

"Man, this is a bad dream," thought Manley out loud.

He wondered if Momma Pearl's hamburgers had been tainted.

"Come. I want to show you something," said Myra as she got out of the car.

As Manley followed her, a bitter wind cut through his clothing, forcing him to shiver involuntarily. Surprisingly, the air was specked with light, blowing snow. They walked slowly amongst the graves and finally stopped in front of a rather nondescript, ordinary- looking headstone.

"Read it," commanded Myra.

Manley began to read. "Lila Mae Adkins. Born

132

April 12, 1928. Died June 6, 1946. Now wait a minute! Lila Mae ain't dead. Today is 1948, and I saw her jest last week, and she's fit as a fiddle. But this here gravestone says she died two years ago. That don't make sense."

"She did, Manley. Not physically, but spiritually. And you helped kill her. In fact, you were her chief judge and executioner."

"You ain't layin' that on my shoulders. Don't nobody much like Lila Mae. Why, she ain't nothing but poor white-trash."

"That's just the thing that killed her spirit, Manley."

"What's that?"

"Your attitude. Your spirit. If you and your wolf pack down at the Coal Dust had treated her halfway decently, she'd still be alive today."

"She deserved ever'thing she got. Besides, like I said, she's alive and well as far as I can tell."

Myra shook her head in disbelief. Somehow, she must make Manley understand. Somehow, she must show him the importance of the decision he must make tonight. They continued to walk through the graveyard as Myra pointed out the other people whose spirits Manley had helped to kill. Through it all, he seemed untouched, unfazed, and un-repentant. That's because Manley had convinced himself that this was some kind of bad dream or a bad case of alco-holic hallucination.

"I'm gittin' bored with this, Myra," Manley said at last. "Can we git home?"

"If you wish, but I have one more stop to make."

"If you must, but make it quick."

They returned to the car. As Myra drove, Manley dozed off. Perhaps I'll wake up back at the Coal Dust, he thought, just before drifting off to sleep. But that did not happen. When he awoke, they were parked in front of a large brick

133

building.

"Well, where we at now, Miss Myra Hallucination?"

"We're at the spiritual hospital. I want to show you some 'friends' of yours that you've helped put here."

Without further explanation, Myra led him into the building and down a long, dimly-lit corridor. The place had that heavy medicine smell of a hospital. It was a smell that always turned Manley's stomach. Myra stopped in front of a door and motioned for Manley to look inside. The room was dark, being lit only by a street lamp through the window. On the bed lay a woman in her mid-fifties who was obviously gravely ill.

"It's Momma Pearl! What's she doin' here?" said Manley in surprise.

"You're killing her, Manley. Don't you understand? Physically, she may be OK, but on the inside, she's dying. With every drink you take and every fight you start, you are killing her."

"Look, Myra, this here dream has gone on long enough. I ain't never raised my hand to Momma Pearl, and I ain't never hurt her, and you know it. Besides, what I do with my life is my business. And right now all I want to do is wake up so I can go back to sleep in my own bed."

"We have one last patient to visit."

"You ain't gonna bore me with the future, are ya?"

"No, Manley. Even I am not privileged to see that. But I want you to know that what I am showing you is for your own good. Everybody in life gets a second chance. In fact, everybody gets several second chances. But there comes a time, and your time has come, when a person comes down to their last second chance."

"So?"

"So, Manley, if you don't change your ways — now — tonight, there will be no more second chances for you, and

134

sadly to say, I will cross you off my list. Forever."

Manley thought he was in the middle of one of the most unusual and disturbing dreams he had ever experienced. But he did not believe in guardian angels. And he did not believe in second chances. No. A man made his own way, created his own luck, in this world. Sure he hadn't been very lucky up until now, but things were going to change. Just wait and see. Tomorrow his luck would change — if he could but escape from this never-ending nightmare in which he had somehow become entrapped.

"Go ahead," said Manley, "Show me yer last patient and then git me back to the Coal Dust."

Myra led him down the hall to another room. Inside, a man lay on a bed. He was heavily bandaged and struggled to breathe. A tube ran down his throat, and the monitors pulsated with every feeble beat of his heart.

"Go on," said Myra, "take a closer look."

Manley approached the bed until he could clearly see who the man was. The patient's breathing was labored, and he had dried blood in one corner of his mouth. When Manley recognized who it was, he turned in disgust and nearly stormed from the room.

"It's Gene. It's Gene Morgan. Do you think I care two shakes about him?"

"Manley, he —"

Manley would not let her explain. If she was trying to prove something by showing him a sick and dying Gene Morgan, she had better think twice.

"We're outta here, Myra. Ya hear me? Outta here. The dream's over. Right now. So take me back and don't show me anymore of yer pity shows. I don't care ta see 'em."

Myra looked at him. Her eyes filled with sadness and pain. She started to say something, but held back.

"As you wish," she finally said. She quickly waved her

hand in front of Manley's face. The movement was so sudden and unexpected that it made him blink. Instantly, he was back at the Coal Dust with a half-empty bottle of beer in his hand.

"I said, who are you talkin' to, Manley?" asked Andy.

Manley blinked and leaned back on his stool. Looking around, he saw the usual crew — Earl, Clem, Jessup — sitting in their usual places. But Myra was gone.

"Oh, no one, Andy, no one. I was jest dreamin' out loud, I suppose."

At that moment, the door to the tavern swung open. Gene Morgan entered the room.

* * * * * * * *

Ten years later, Manley rose from his bunk and surveyed the recreation area outside his window. A new prisoner had arrived today. He had been placed in the cell directly across from Manley. He was a young kid, and it was probably his first time behind bars.

Gene was dead; had been for ten years. That night at the Coal Dust, Manley and Gene had a fight. That was when Manley shot him. If it had not been for the thirteen gunshot wounds, he might have plead self-defense or manslaughter. Instead, he received life without parole. No mercy. No luck.

Momma Pearl had died eight years ago, and Corina and Teddy had moved away to another state. And he had not had a drink in ten years. Consequently, Manley had plenty of time to soberly think things over. But it was an exercise in futility and frustration. He had concluded long ago that the past was as dead as those gravestones Myra had shown him in his dream. There was nothing he could do about the past now. And seemingly, there was nothing he could do about the future, either. And so he sat in his cell, day by

136

day, slowly rotting away.

As he continued to look out the window, he could hear the clank of keys unlocking the big door down the hallway. It opened with a thud, and he could hear footsteps coming down the corridor. It was the sound of guard's footsteps. Their boots made a distinctive sound. The footsteps stopped in front of his cell, and he heard a voice.

"Jeffrey, we need to have a little talk."

That voice was familiar. Manley turned to see a female guard. She was talking to the new prisoner across the hall.

"Myra?" he said, looking intently at this new, yet familiar, female guard. She did not respond, but continued to talk to the young prisoner. "Myra, is that you?" Still no response. "Myra, for goodness sakes, if that's you, please talk to me."

Finally, the guard turned. It was Myra. Perhaps, she could bring him some words of hope. After all, he was ready now to change his ways. He just needed a little help. However, her reply was like a slap in his face.

"Why should I waste my time with you, Manley? You are no longer on my list. You have already had your last second chance."

She turned, unlocked the cell, and went in to counsel the new, young inmate. Manley was left completely ignored, standing at the door to his cell. Manley glanced away for a second. When he looked back, the cell across from him was empty. He knew that eventually Myra would return the young man to his cell. He found himself hoping that this young man, unlike himself, would take full advantage of his only last second chance.

♠ ♠

The Turn of a Screw
By Pappy Kincaid

Pappy Kincaid, a crusty old mountaineer, is a storytellin' friend of mine. He couldn't let me write a book without getting in his two-cents worth of storytellin'. So, here's his ruminations about his visit to the big city.

♠ ♠

Recently, I went to visit Tom, my nephew, in the big city. Now, it doesn't make any difference which big city. They're all alike in my book. If you've seen one skyscraper, you've seen 'em all. Of course, that's what city-folks say about mountains, but they're sorely mistaken in that regards.

Anyway, there was one thing Tom showed me that caught my fancy. We went down to the local mall. (That's another thing that looks the same no matter where ya go.) Outside, down on one corner, cars were lined up for over a block. I figured that someone was givin' away free car washes, or motor oil, or something like that. However, when we got closer, it looked more like free inspections. Tom pulled his car over to the curb and parked.

"This is what I wanted to show you," he said.

The cars seemed to be goin' through a series of inspection stations. At the first station, folks would come scurryin' out and about the car, stickin' different types of electronic devices into the passenger compartment. At another station, another team was crawlin' around under the hood. At the third station, another group was nosin' around in the trunk. My, my, I thought, they certainly do inspections up big in the city. Why, back home on Loop Creek ol' Eddie Brown would look your car over, turn on your headlights, blow your horn, and slap a new sticker on your windshield. The whole process took about five minutes, if you don't count all the time spent jaw-bonin'.

"What's all the fuss about?" I asked.

"This is a car stereo competition," proclaimed Tom.

"A what?"

"A car stereo competition. We're seeing who has the best car stereo. We have regional and even national competitions. Of course, there's a division for small trucks, too."

"You're kiddin' me. A car stereo competition."

"No kidding, look over here. At the first station, they're checking your sound quality in the passenger compartment. You want to make sure that the sound is uniform throughout. Don't want any dead spots, you know."

Right. It would be a shame for someone with their ear down by the gear shift, pickin' up something they dropped in the floor, to miss out on a high note or two. Sounded to me like some folks at this competition had some dead spots in their heads.

"And at the other two stations," Tom continued to explain, "they're inspecting the overall neatness of your installation."

No kiddin', I thought. Just leave it up to a bunch of Americans to make a competition out of something as simple as a radio. Tom explained to me later that you really can't get a radio for your vehicle anymore — it's a sound system. It's an insult these days to tell someone that you like their radio.

139

While watchin' the activity at the car stereo competition, I came to the conclusion that we live in a country where folks either a) got too much time on their hands, b) got too much money in their pockets, c) have very low self-esteem, or d) all of the above. Why is it we're always twistin' simple things into heated competitions — tryin' to see who's the best at everything? What ever happened to the simple pleasures of life? Why, folks can't even eat and drink and enjoy their food any more without worryin' about fat-grams and fiber and all of that malarkey. It's a pity that we've even turned walkin' into a moral obligation. And unnecessary competition is the culprit.

In my mind, this constant competition is a bad thing. For example, back on Loop Creek, there are only two reasons for walkin'. One is to get to where you're goin' and the other is to enjoy the scenery along the way. And the *only* reason for *ever* runnin' that I can think of is to avoid one of Jasper's rabid hound dogs. But in the city, I saw all these people runnin' and joggin' around with pained looks on their faces like someone was stickin' 'em with an ice pick. And where were they goin'? Nowhere. They were just runnin' round in circles or up the block and back. And were they enjoyin' themselves? It didn't look like it to me. Even the walkers looked like they had lost their sense of joy with all this competition that's been foisted on them. Seems like everybody's tryin' to live longer, be skinnier, look handsomer. Well, in my book, ain't nobody winnin', and we're wastin' a lot of time, money, and energy a-tryin'!

Anyway, before I could mingle with these poor, overpaid, under-worked, attention-seekin', stereo-star wannabes, Tom took me over to meet his friend Brian. Brian was a friendly sort of guy in his late twenties or early thirties. He had a truck in the competition.

140

"Brian," said Tom, "why don't you show Pappy here your sound system."

Brain proceeded to show me all of his gear and how it worked, but all his talk about equalizers and frequencies and decibels and woofers and tweeters only made my eyes glaze over. The one thing that did catch my attention was the cost. He had $12,000 worth of electronic gear in his truck — $12,000 to play a song? Come on. Why, for that much money back on Loop Creek, I could hire Clem and Jessup and their entire fiddle-playin' crew for a whole year or two.

Tom went on to tell me that ol' Brain had won the local competition the year before and had advanced to the regionals where he lost by two points. If he had won the regionals, he would have advanced to the national finals. Imagine bein' the grand national car stereo champion. Wouldn't that make your mother proud? Anyway, he lost by two points. You see, as Tom had explained, part of the judgin' is based on neatness. You've got to have all your wires and speakers and such all neat and pretty. Well, ol' Brian failed in that regard. You see, his speakers were mounted with four screws. On one speaker, the slots on the heads of three of those screws were pointin' east and west, but the slot on the fourth screw was pointin' north and south. And for that, the judges deducted three points. Except for one loose screw — one little quarter-turn — Brian would have won.

I think ol' Brain should compete for the national loose-screw award. (They have one, ya know.) I'm sure his speaker ain't the only thing in that truck with a screw or two loose — especially with Brian behind the wheel.

Think about it.

141

♠ ♠ ♠ ♠ ♠ ♠ ♠ ♠ ♠ ♠ ♠ ♠ ♠ ♠

The Christmas Play
That Never Was

♠ ♠ ♠ ♠ ♠ ♠ ♠ ♠ ♠ ♠ ♠ ♠ ♠ ♠ ♠

Have you ever been handed a task in life that was beyond your abilities? Now, I'm not talking about making a sales quota or keeping your house plants from withering away. Potty training your new puppy doesn't count either. What I'm asking is have you ever been assigned a task that sent fear-bumps down your spine and caused you to lie awake at night having serious doubts about your self-worth? Well, I was given such a task one year. It was a Christmas I shall never forget, and in some respects, hope to never relive. It was the Christmas when some bright, thoughtful person on the church youth committee decided that I, Mrs. Carol Miller, was just perfect for the director of the annual Christmas play. It's the type of job you cannot gracefully refuse, but it's also the kind of job that can seriously test your Christianity. Anyone who has been there knows what I'm saying is true.

Now, I'm not talking about a Christmas play for little kids. That's a piece of cake. They can mess up their lines and do all sorts of stupid things, and everybody thinks they're cute. I'm talking about teenagers — fourteen, fifteen, even sixteen years old. These are the ones whose parents are always asking them to act their age, meaning they are expected to act like adults. But do you want to know a secret? They **are** acting their age — young, wild, and untamable. They're only fourteen for goodness sakes, but so much is expected of them. And one of the biggest expectations is that their annual Christmas play is not only professional and entertaining, but also poignant and spiritually moving. Man, what a tall order to fill. That's why the director is on the hot spot. She must guide and counsel (translated: ride herd on) these darling youths to produce and to produce on cue — no flubbed lines, exotic scenery, a fast-paced plot, low budget, limited rehearsal time, laughs and pathos — all in the same play. Even Steven Spielberg would be tested.

Let me take you back to that fateful year. The date is not important because the scenario is always the same. But that year, everything that a director fears might happen, did happen. It was the year of the Christmas Play That Never Was.

It began normally. Announcements were made shortly after Labor Day that we were having a Christmas play for the older youth. Kids were asked to volunteer for parts. This play, as all play announcements go, was going to be the biggest and best the church youth had ever done. It was going to be more fun and adventure than a young person could possibly experience. It was going to be an opportunity of a lifetime. (Father, forgive us. Sometimes play directors cross over the line between hype and outright lying.)

By Thanksgiving, despite repeated calls for volunteers and bribes of pizza parties, only two kids had signed up. One was Thelma, a straight-A student who was — how can I say this politely? Well, she was a straight-A student who was a straight-A student. That's it. She was shy and socially backward. She had few real friends. And quite frankly, she had no flair for the dramatic. Although she could probably memorize the whole play in one afternoon, she had no voice. No matter how much she was coached, she was never going to be heard beyond the second row of pews.

The second volunteer was Philip, the class clown. I believe he signed up just to torture me. He was the kind of kid who had great potential if it could only be focused on one activity. But Philip was never focused on anything except the unending task of being noticed. There was nothing in the counselor's manuals about how to handle a Philip. No method or approach seemed to work with him. He could not be moved with sweet talk, he ignored threats, and he couldn't care less about being bribed with pizza. His sole goal in life was to cause trouble — not big trouble, mind you — just the constant water-dripping-in-the-middle-of-the-night type trouble.

At any rate, Thanksgiving was quickly approaching, and I had no cast. So I resorted to the tried and true method. I began drafting. By Turkey Day, everybody had a part and everybody knew when the first practice was going to be held. And everybody knew how precious little time we had to pull the play together.

On that first practice day, I arrived with great expectations. Expectations that were soon to end in disappointment. Half of the cast failed to show up, and the other half was in a sour mood. They were milling around aimlessly, waiting for me to attempt to take charge. The practice went something like the following.

"OK, OK," I said. "Let's all settle down and get started." I waited for everybody to congregate around the stage. "Tonight, we are going to start practicing our Christmas play. The title is 'Angels, Shepherds and Wise Men Three'."

April and Carrie, the thirteen-year-old Thompson twins, said in unison in a singsong voice, "Boring!"

I tried to ignore and work around their comment. At

that point, I noticed Will, who had been absent when I had handed out parts the week before.

"Will, my friend," I started. He was tall and muscular and perfect for the part I had assigned him. I just knew he would be satisfied with it. "I want you to be Gabriel."

"Who's he, Mrs. Miller?"

Will was always polite. He always called me Mrs. Miller even when I encouraged him to call me Carol.

"An angel," I said.

"I ain't gonna be no angel for ya, Mrs. Miller," he said in a deep bass voice. "Angels are sissies."

His simple statement sparked a mutiny.

"Me neither," said another boy.

And little Katie chipped in, "Yeah, and I don't want to be a shepherd, neither."

"But Katie. . ." I started to explain, but it was no use. The grumbling spread rapidly throughout the group. I was sure it was just a nervous reaction to the reality of being trapped in a Christmas play. I wanted to assure them that all of us were scared, even me, but we had to face our fears together. I was contemplating telling them that this would be a growing experience, and that someday they would look back on this and be glad they had been part of a great performance, a great team effort. But what came out of my mouth was a shrill, "Now wait a minute! Can't I get a little cooperation from this crew? If nobody wants to do their part, how are we going to have a play?"

"Let's not have a play this year," said Philip.

I knew he had been waiting for the opportune time to spring his ambush. Everybody chimed in, "Yeah, no play." Philip certainly had leadership qualities, but he was about to lead this play practice right down the tubes.

"You know, Mrs. Miller, every year it's the same old play," said Will in his slow, deep voice. "Wise men, angels,

145

shepherds."

"And nobody learns their lines," said Maggie.

"And nobody hears what we say, anyway," said Thelma, joining the revolt with her soft voice.

"And nobody really cares, either," summed up Philip.

The whole turn of events left me speechless. I was not sure how to counter their arguments and regain control of the practice. While I was considering my next move, Adrian, a very bright and talented young girl, offered an alternative.

"Hey, gang," she said, "I have an idea. Let's give them real entertainment this year. You know, Show Biz. Bright lights. Jazzy songs. A little rap and jive dancing. Maybe even a little — "

"Adrian! This is church. Let's keep it dignified," I protested.

"That's just it, Carol," said Adrian. "Look at the competition — movies, TV. If we don't offer something that catches the ear or eye, nobody is going to pay any attention to us."

Needless to say, most of that first practice was spent regaining control of the situation. After all, who was the director, me or them? After much persuasion and a little arm twisting, everybody grudgingly agreed to dispense with the rap and jive and settled on the more conservative 'Angels, Shepherds, and Wise Men Three'. But by that time, we had no time for practice. The next day, disaster struck. I was getting ready to fix dinner when the phone rang.

"Carol, do you have a minute to meet me down at the church?" It was Nancy Blake, Thelma's mother.

"Sure, Nancy. What's up?"

"Well, we've got a problem."

"What is it?"

146

"I'd rather not talk about it on the phone. I'll have to show you. Will you meet me at church in say — fifteen minutes?"

"Sure," I said, puzzled by the urgency of her request.

When I arrived at the church, Nancy was waiting for me on the front steps. We had a neat little church with hardwood siding, painted white. It was perhaps eighty or ninety years old and had large, drafty windows that creaked during the winter snows and magnified the summer heat. The church sat at the foot of a mountain that towered above the steeple, and directly in front of the church lay a railroad track. At one time, the trains had run continuously past the little church, carrying black coal to the steel mills in the north. But in recent years, there was very little activity. An occasional train in the morning and perhaps one in the late afternoon was all that passed by anymore.

"Wow," said Nancy as I got out of my car, "I thought you were never going to get here."

I looked at my watch. It had taken me nine minutes.

"What's going on Nancy?"

"Just look."

Nancy pointed to the adjacent hillside where four abandoned houses were rotting away. They had once been part of the coal boom, but they were now very much rundown. They had been abandoned for as long as I could remember, and I had lived on Loop Creek for almost thirty years.

"The abandoned houses?" I asked. "I don't see anything unusual."

"Just wait and you'll see," insisted Nancy.

We stood on the church steps for about five minutes, gazing at the ruins on the nearby hillside. Finally, it happened. A huge, dark figure emerged from the second house from the right. It was facing away from us as it came through the door, but almost immediately turned our way.

147

Stretching out its long arms, it gave out a long, loud yawn. It was a man. At least, I thought it was a man. He was tall, perhaps six-foot-six or more. His hair, matted with dirt, hung below his shoulders. His beard was long and frizzed-out, giving him the appearance of a madman. He appeared to be wearing layers of tattered clothing that made him look even larger than he was.

As I stared at this strange figure, my eyes were drawn to his face. In that moment, we made eye contact. At least, that was my perception. His black, emotionless eyes appeared to look directly at me, holding me captive in his gaze. It was as if he was looking though my eyes into the very depths of my being, and what I felt in that moment was contempt — utter loathing and contempt for his filthy, somehow menacing presence. Fear overcame me, and I was forced to look away.

"He's staring at me," I whispered to Nancy. I was unable to look up.

"I know. That's what I want to talk to you about."

"Can we go inside?"

"Sure," said Nancy. She unlocked the door to the church, and we went inside and sat on the first row of pews near the podium.

"Who is he?" I asked.

"No one knows. He just showed up a couple of days ago and setup housekeeping in those old houses."

"Is he dangerous?"

"Don't know, Carol, but he has been snooping around the church."

"No."

"Yes. Clarence saw him late yesterday standing next to the storage shed 'round the side over there. When he saw Clarence, he ran off up the hill into the woods."

"What time was that?" I asked.

"About five."

"Nancy," I said, growing more and more concerned, "that's when I had all the kids in here for play practice."

"I know. That's why I wanted you to know about him. As far as I know, he hasn't hurt anyone but —"

There was a noise at the back of the sanctuary. Nancy and I looked up to see the stranger, standing in the doorway, filling it with his bulk. The sun was behind him, and his frizzled-out hair cast a long and wild shadow. He was so huge and ominous that I found myself letting out a quick gasp as I rose to my feet. Almost immediately, the stranger turned and, without saying a word, walked quickly away. Instinctively, and perhaps foolishly, we followed him. The front door slammed shut. When we arrived there, we caught only a glimpse of him hurrying down the railroad tracks.

"He's certainly spooky," exclaimed Nancy.

"He certainly is," I said as my knees began to shake uncontrollably. "He certainly is. And he's certainly making himself at home around the church."

Nancy closed and locked the church door as we made our way to our cars. "I don't want to be an alarmist, Carol, but if I were you, I'd keep an eye out for that guy."

"Yes," I said, "I certainly will."

My mind was so preoccupied by this unexpected turn of events that I almost didn't hear Nancy's next statement. It was a statement that, once fully understood, sent another wave of fear coursing through my body.

"Oh, by the way, Carol," she said, "we've move your play up a week."

"You've what! But I —"

"Carol," Nancy said in her most authoritative voice, "we have the cantata, the children's program, the Sunday School party, the caroling, the food baskets and all. The only way we can fit it all in is to reschedule your play."

"But I won't have time to practice," I protested.

Nancy smiled. "We all have the utmost confidence in you, Carol. Don't worry. You can do it. You've got a great bunch of kids."

Great, I thought, not only did I have a mysterious, menacing-looking stranger running around the neighborhood, but I had also lost a precious week of practice time. And this play was still at the starting line. The next practice had better be a good one. I called an emergency practice for Thursday afternoon right after school, but only four kids showed up, and they didn't have any of the key parts. The next regularly scheduled practice was for Saturday afternoon. That's when it dawned on me — I had only one week left! I was beginning to panic. My whole social standing in the community rested on this performance. No one had ever had a Christmas play bomb, but it looked as if Carol Miller — me — was going to make history right alongside the Titanic and Edsel!

The play practice on Saturday only confirmed my fears. We were right in the middle of practice when it all fell apart again. Philip was in the middle of reading his part when it happened.

"Nathan . . . my son . . . I have a task . . . for you."

"Philip," I said, interrupting his simply dreadful reading. I knew he has doing it on purpose. "Don't you know your part yet? The play is next week."

"Well, uh... oh, uh... I've been busy."

"But, Philip, we've been counting on you, and you have the biggest part."

"Well, uh, gee," he said with a slight grin, "maybe you should get someone else."

"We can't Philip. There's not enough time. You'll just have to tough it out."

He began to read his part again. This time he did a

150

much better job. "Nathan, my son, I have a task for you."

"I can guess what you want me to do, Father. You want me to go to Bethle. . ." Maggie stopped in mid-sentence, put her hands on her hips, and looked me straight in the eye. "Mom, do I have to be a boy?"

"Yes, Maggie," I said, "we're short on boys this year. We barely have enough for the wise men."

"But I don't want to be a boy."

That was Will's cue. "And I don't want to be Gabriel, either."

I knew they were only testing me — again — for the umpteenth time. And I knew if I didn't squelch this mutiny fast, another play practice would be lost. I was just getting ready to launch into my stern-agitated-and-on-the-verge-of-screaming routine when Thelma screeched and pointed to the windows. Coming from Thelma, it was more like a squeal than a scream, but it got everybody's attention. Her squeal was soon followed by several other gasps and exclamations. At the window stood the tall, hairy, filthy stranger. His dirty hands were pressed against the pane, and his grubby nose was flattened against it, too. He stood there for a moment, towering at the window and peering at us with his empty, black eyes. His seemingly sudden appearance and his menacing looks unnerved everybody.

"He's going to kill us!" one of the girls shouted.

Realizing he had been discovered, the stranger blinked his eyes, quickly withdrew from the window, and raced away. As Will and Philip ran to protect the front door, I went to the window to see where he went and caught a glimpse of him climbing the hillside behind the church. After that bit of excitement, it took some time to get everybody settled down. Kids were racing around the sanctuary, looking out every available window. Some of the boys took to jumping from behind the curtains and the piano, scaring the girls and keeping the whole situation agitated.

"He followed me down the railroad tracks when I came here," announced Thelma quietly.

"Why didn't you tell me before now?" I asked.

"I didn't think it was that important," said Thelma.

From that point on, the discussion centered around the mystery man. Who was he and why was he stalking the church? Another play practice wasted. Another day lost. As the kids left church that night, I made sure each one was escorted to their car and safely home.

That night I lay awake in bed and thought about Dora Jean. Dora Jean, the deacon's wife. Dora Jean, the deacon's wife, who did everything with a dramatic flare. Dora Jean, the deacon's wife, who grabbed all the attention. Dora Jean, the deacon's wife, who garnered all the praise. Last year as director, she had produced a Christmas extravaganza complete with spotlights, new costumes, brightly painted plywood scenery, and live animals. She even had a live Baby Jesus. It was her granddaughter Stacy. But being the granddaughter of Dora Jean, the deacon's wife, automatically qualified her for the part regardless of her sex.

I had wondered how I was going to top Dora Jean's (the deacon's wife) play. Stacy was a year-and-a-half old now — much to old for the part — and there were no little babies in the church this year. To make matters worse, all of the senior leadership in the youth group had moved on to college, and I was stuck with Philip, Adrian, and Thelma, the rogue, the radical, and the recluse, respectively. I was facing a disaster of Biblical proportions and could find no way out. It was too late to resign, too late to start over with a new cast — too late, too late, too late. That night I fell asleep with those two little words echoing in my head — "too late." My social status on Loop Creek was about to come crashing down.

On the day of the play, I planned one last rehearsal that afternoon. I was hoping against hope that I could pull this fiasco together. The whole crew was waiting for me when I arrived — the whole crew except Philip and Adrian, my costars. Anger began to boil up inside me. I expected Philip to cause trouble, but I never expected him to desert me. Without him and Adrian, the play would have to be canceled. There were no other options. Inside, another discovery confirmed my hopelessness. The costumes were missing. They had been left in two big boxes behind the makeshift curtains, but now they were nowhere to be found.

"What are we going to do, Mrs. Miller?" asked Thelma.

"Punt," said Carrie and April, the Thompson twins.

"Yes, I believe you're right, punt," I confirmed. "I guess we can sing a few songs and read some scripture, but I don't think we'll be doing any play."

For the first time, I saw true disappointment on their faces.

"Mrs. Miller," called Will from the back of the church. "Come here. I've found something."

We all raced to the rear door where Will stood, pointing to a huge, muddy footprint. It was a footprint that could only belong to one person — the mysterious stranger. My anger toward Philip and Adrian melted away into concern. We had been robbed.

The lights on the Christmas tree in the sanctuary twinkled silently as the pews began to fill. The main lights were off, and the tree provided a warm glow to the smiling faces that were filtering in. The air was punctuated by friendly small talk and occasional light laughter. All was right with the world. In a few minutes, the curtains would be drawn and the play — the social highlight of Loop Creek's Christmas season — would begin. Little did the congregation suspect that we had no play to offer. Behind the curtains, huddled amongst the cast, I was on the verge of a breakdown. We had been unable to find Philip and Adrian. The costumes were still missing. And to make matters worse, the pastor had not arrived to provide us any advice and counsel. And there was Dora Jean, the deacon's wife, sitting on the front row.

As the time for the service to start approached, I decided on a strategy. I was going to march out on the stage, apologize to the congregation, turn the service over to the pastor, and with my head held high, walk right down the aisle and out the door, never to be seen again. That was my plan.

"Mrs. Miller," said Will, "look."

Standing at the rear door was a wise man. A flowing purple robe covered his shoulders. His head was garnished with a most exquisite, gold-painted, aluminum-foil crown. His salt-and-pepper beard was well trimmed, giving him a truly regal appearance. His face was beaming a broad smile, and his eyes were alive with life. It was the mysterious stranger. Before I could react, Philip and Adrian pushed the wise man aside, their arms laden with the lost costume boxes.

"Quick!" called Adrian to the cast. "Put on a costume. Anything!"

"But — " I said, pointing to the stranger.

"That's Denver," said Philip. "He just wants to be in the play."

"He what?" I said. "What play?"

"Our play, Mrs. Miller, our play," said Adrian. "He's never been in a Christmas play before, so we wrote one for him."

"You what?" I said, totally confused.

"Carol," said Philip in his most reassuring voice, "we have it all figured out, so you're just gonna have to trust us.

We've spent the whole afternoon gettin' Denver cleaned up and makin' a costume that fits. So, you've just got to let him have a part."

"But that's just it. We don't have a play," I protested.

"Oh, yes, we do," said Adrian. "Just watch."

The congregation was singing an opening hymn. Play time was upon us. I had no other choice but to go along with whatever scheme they had devised. As Adrian and Philip huddled with the cast, I retreated to an offstage chair to watch "my" masterpiece unfold. The cast was still scurrying around the stage when the curtain was drawn. Philip and Will turned and looked at the audience, apparently in surprise. For an awkward moment, nobody seemed to know what to do. Finally, the two boys stepped to the front of the stage and stood with their arms folded, staring at the floor. Will, in his slow, deep voice, began to speak to the audience.

"Ladies and Gentlemen, before we go any further, I have an announcement to make. Mrs. Miller said we'd have to do this because, like Pontius Pilot, she's washing her hands of the whole mess." My heart began to fail me. Will continued, "I hate to say this, but we are not gonna have a play this year. I know you all are expecting a play tonight, but we're not doing one. We've had a few problems, you see. We couldn't find a good script. No one would come to play practice. Everybody wanted to do their own thing. So, we don't have a play for you tonight and we're sorry."

"Yeah," said Philip, "no play. And here we are on stage. I don't know quite what to do."

"Maybe," said Will, "we can sing some songs. Would you all out there like to sing some songs?"

"Or maybe," continued Philip hesitantly, "we could read some scripture, or. . ."

At that moment, Adrian came forward to join the two

155

boys on stage.

"Wait a minute," she said. "Do you mean we're not having a play? Weren't we supposed to do 'Strangers in Bethlehem'?"

"No," corrected Will, "It was 'Baby Jesus and the Inn Keeper'."

"I don't know," said Philip. "I lost my part."

"Hold on guys," interrupted Adrian. "Since we are all here, and we don't have a play, why don't we just show everybody what happened. I'm sure they want a detailed explanation for this disaster."

They all looked at each other for a moment.

"OK!" said Philip. He turned to the audience. "Give us a minute, and we'll try to reconstruct the scene of the crime."

The curtain began to close, but just as it did, Adrian stuck her head back through the curtain.

"Scene II coming up!" she announced with two fingers held high in the air.

As the curtain closed, I ran over to Philip and Adrian.

"Cute. But what are you going to do now?" I asked.

"Carol," said Philip, "just how many years do you think it takes to learn how to do a Christmas play?"

"We've been at this for years," added Adrian. "Do you think we don't know what to do by now?"

There was no time to argue. Play time was upon us again. The curtain was opening, and I retreated offstage.

What unfolded after that was a work of sheer ad-lib genius. With Adrian pretending to be me and everybody else playing themselves, the entire cast reconstructed the events of the past few weeks. Every practice and every failure were recounted in a light and humorous way. Even Denver played himself, sneaking outside and peering through the windows. The entire performance looked slick

156

and totally rehearsed. But I wondered how it would end. Finally, Philip, Adrian, and Will once again stood on an empty stage.

"Well," said Philip, "now you know why we don't have a play for you tonight."

"Yeah," said Will, "we goofed off so much that we ran out of time."

"Yeah," said Philip, "we really are sorry."

"Wait!" exclaimed Adrian. "I have an idea. The Christmas story is a simple story. Let's just give it to them straight."

"Huh?" said Will.

"Let's just go back to the original script!" said Adrian.

"What original script?" asked Will and Philip.

"THE original script. The Bible."

"Oh, yeah, you're right," said the boys in unison.

The curtain closed again. When it reopened, the cast had assembled a manger scene. Will walked to the podium. In a deep, dignified voice, he began to read the Christmas story from the Bible. As he read, the other kids pantomimed the scenes — Mary and Joseph with the Baby, the shepherds and the angels, and the wise men. Yes, the wise men. As Will read, Denver, starring in his very first Christmas play and towering above the rest of the cast, led the wise men down the center aisle and onto the stage where a plastic Baby Jesus lay. There were actually tears running down his cheeks as he bowed and placed his gift at the foot of the manger. I thought back to our first encounter when he had seemed so menacing. Gone forever were those cold, emotionless eyes that had haunted me so much.

Top that one, Dora Jean!

The End of the World
By Little Johnny

My stupid cat was missin'. Either that or the rapture had come. The preacher had been talkin' a lot lately about the rapture, about how Jesus was comin' back someday to take all of his people — all the saved people — home to heaven with Him. When that happens, so the preacher said, the only ones left here on the earth will be sinners and workers of abominations. And then the whole world will be plunged into a terrible tribulation filled with plagues and wars and all sorts of mayhem. And, of course, all the sinners will end up burnin' in hell with the devil and all of his demons. The scary part, at least for all the sinners, is that it could happen at any time — day or night. Jesus would just step out on the clouds of glory and call his people home, and all the folks left behind would be destined to burn in the fires of hell. I guess, sometimes, in order to make a man fit for heaven, the preacher's first got to scare hell out of him. And the preacher did a real good job of doin' just that from time to time. That's why at that particular moment, I chose to believe my stupid cat was missin' instead of the rapture havin' come. 'Cause if the rapture had come, and I was left behind, then that meant I was a sinner indeed, and there was no hope for me from that day forward. I'd always thought sinners to be great company for havin' a little fun with from time to time, but I didn't want to spend the rest of my eternity with them. You wouldn't either.

158

I'd been out in the woods, scroungin' up blackberries for Gramma Goldie to make into a cobbler. When I arrived home, the whole house was empty. Normally, Cleo, my Siamese cat, would be sleepin' on the doormat, but she wasn't there. I felt the doormat for a sign of heat, but there was none, indicatin' she had not been there for some time.

"Hi, Mom, I'm home."

No answer. That was strange. Mom was always home in the afternoons. Brother Tom always needed his nap. But Mom was not home today, and neither were my younger sister and brothers. The house was completely empty. That's when I thought about the rapture. And that's when I thought about Cleo. If the rapture had actually happened, I figured God would take all the house pets, too. After all, they weren't sinners, and only sinner's were gonna be left behind. So, if Cleo was still around, then chances were Mom and the kids were, too.

I searched all through the house. I looked in all the closets. I even looked in the cubbyhole under the basement steps. But Cleo was not there. The house was completely empty — and silent. I'd never heard it so silent in my whole life. Usually, there was always someone laughin', or cryin', or even snorin'. But on that day, the house was filled with an eerie silence. It was then I came to the only conclusion a good God-fearin' sinner could come to. The rapture had come, and I was left behind. And without Gramma Goldie, I had all of these delicious blackberries in my bucket that were gonna go to waste.

I ran over to Gramma Goldie's house to make sure the Lord had taken her. When I got there, I wasn't disappointed. Her house was empty, too. There was a pot of green beans sittin' on the stove, just waitin' for someone to turn the burner on. That's when I realized how lost and alone I was really gonna be. Without a mess of Gramma

Goldie's green beans from time to time, life really wouldn't be worth livin'.

I ran out to the fillin' station, expectin' to see Grit or Hodgekins out there. I knew the Lord would take Eddie Brown. He probably had a golden fillin' station waitin' for him in heaven. Then again, probably not. Eddie would have been satisfied just to spend the rest of eternity right there on Loop Creek. But Hodgekins and Grit were another matter. I just knew one of them was a sinner and the other was a hypocrite. I just hadn't figured out which one was which. I fully expected to see at least one of them wanderin' around the fillin' station in a daze, wonderin' where Eddie had disappeared to. Boy, was I in for a big surprise and bone-chillin' disappointment.

The fillin' station was completely empty, too. To beat it all, it was all locked-up with a "Closed" sign in the window. It was as if Eddie knew the Lord was comin' and closed up shop before he left. That's when I really started to panic. I mean, if I had to spend eternity in hell, at least Grit and Hodgekins would have made some tolerable company. But it looked as if the Lord had taken them, too. Was I the only sinner on Loop Creek? You don't know what a blow that thought was to my ego.

I stood there at the fillin' station, noticin' how quiet things were. There was no traffic on the road. There were no voices in the air. There were no birds singin' in the trees. The rapture had really come. I had really been left behind. And I really was all alone. Just then, I heard a screen door slam shut. The sound came from across the creek in the direction of Clarence's place. I ran over and jumped up on the wall next to the fillin' station to get a better look, and there was ol' Clarence wanderin' around in his yard. Well, praise the Lord. I wasn't the only sinner on Loop Creek.

Whoa! Wait a minute, I thought. Maybe the rapture

160

hadn't come. After all, Clarence was a deacon down at the Baptist Church. Surely, if anyone would go to heaven in the rapture, it would be old Clarence. I ran down the road and across the creek and breathlessly plopped down in Clarence's yard on his favorite tree stump.

"Boy, Clarence, am I glad to see you."

"Ya are? How come?"

"I've had a real scare this afternoon. I came home and there was nobody there. Mom, Karen, Tom, Jim — they're all missin'. Even my cat Cleo is gone. And Granny's gone, too. So, I got to thinkin' about what the preacher's been sayin' about the rapture, and I thought — well, I thought that — "

"You thought that the rapture had come," Clarence said, smilin' at me.

"Yeah. Right. And then I went out to the fillin' station and it's closed! Eddie, Grit, and Hodgekins ain't there. That's when I knew I'd been left behind. Well, I was about to panic until I saw you, and then I knew I had nothin' to worry about."

"Why is that?"

"'Cause with you here, Clarence, I knew that the rapture hadn't come."

"What makes you so sure, son?"

"'Cause you're a deacon."

Clarence rubbed his chin and frowned. "You say your family's gone?"

"Yep."

"And your cat's gone?"

"Yep."

"And Eddie's gone?"

"Yep."

"And Grit and Hodgekins are gone?"

"Yep."

161

"And the station's closed?"

"Yep."

"Then what makes you so sure we ain't the only two sinners left on Loop Creek?" Clarence nearly scared the livin' bejeevers out of me with that statement.

"But Clarence, you're a de—"

"A deacon in the Baptist Church," he said, finishin' my sentence. "Boy, don't you ever judge the insides of a man based on his title or position. And don't be more concerned about another man's fate than you are with your own. The way I figure it, if you're right, you and me and old Lucifer are gonna spend a lot of time together. And it ain't gonna be playin' tiddlywinks."

Clarence was scarin' more than the bejeevers out of me now. At that moment, I was lookin' for a hole to crawl into, but I knew Clarence wasn't gonna let me use his miniature coal mine for that purpose. Just then, a car came down the hill, pulled into the grass at Gramma Goldie's place, and a whole gang of folks piled out of the car. It was Uncle Lawrence — and Mom and the kids — and Gramma Goldie. I was never so glad to seem them in all of my short thirteen years of life.

Clarence stuck a straw into his mouth and looked down at me.

"Well," he said, "looks like the end of the world hasn't happened yet. But, mark my word, it will someday, and, son, when it does, you'd better be sure you're ready for it."

I ran across Clarence's wooden bridge, and without looking, darted across the road.

"Boy, oh, boy, am I glad to see you guys," I said, clenchin' Mom's waist as tight as I could.

"Ya are, are ya?" said Uncle Lawrence. "Is that because ya wanna go for a ride in my new convertible?"

"No," I said, breathless from all the excitement of the

162

rapture and the dash across Clarence's bridge. "I thought all of y'all had been rapt—"

Mom interrupted. "Johnny, did you look before runnin' across the road? How many times have I told you, son, you've got to look? You're gonna get run over one of these days."

"Sorry, Mom, I just — "

"Hush, child. I don't want any excuses."

"Yes, ma'am," I said. I was almost sorry I had been so glad to see her just a few minutes earlier.

"Well, boy, do ya want a ride or not?"

"Oh, no, Uncle Lawrence. I can't right now. I've got to find my cat. Mom, have you seen Cleo?"

"She was on the porch when we left. She's probably around here somewhere."

But she wasn't. I looked all through the house again. I searched the nearby hillside, roadside, and creek bank, but Cleo was nowhere in sight. She had simply vanished into thin air, in broad daylight, in the blink of an eye, without a trace. I went out to the fillin' station, but didn't find her there either. But I did discover why the station had been closed. Eddie had broken his arm while play-wrestlin' with Grit. They had whisked him up to the hospital in Oak Hill to get it patched up.

"You fellas seen my cat Cleo?"

"Nope," said Grit. "Been too busy doctorin' Eddie."

"Well, she's just up and disappeared."

"Cats'll do that," said Grit. "They'll wander off for three or four days — sometimes for a week or more — without any warnin', and then one mornin' you'll wake up, and there they are back on your doorstep. I wouldn't worry too much about her none."

"If it makes you feel any better, you can put a sign up here in the window," offered Eddie.

163

"Thanks," I said, "I think I will."

So I went home and Mom helped me make a lost-cat sign that I posted in the window at the fillin' station. It made me feel a little better, but not much. Not knowin' can really eat at ya, especially when it's your very favorite pet that you've had for as long as you can remember.

That evenin' Dad came home from work and joined all of us at the supper table. Everybody was laughin' and talkin'. Everybody except Dad. He handed a newspaper to Mom.

"Here, Jitter, read this. I picked it up at work today. Everybody at the plant's been talkin' about it all day long."

Mom read the headlines, "Loop Creek Possible Sight for Dam." She looked at Dad.

"Go on, keep readin'," he said.

She continued to read. "The Army Corps of Engineers announced today a new water conservation program which calls for a major dam in the southern part of the state. Although a final site has not been selected, officials indicated that a prime candidate is the Loop Creek area. Senator Ralston said —"

"That's enough," said Dad.

"What does that mean?" asked Granny.

"It means," said Dad, "if Loop Creek is picked, we'll have to move. They're plannin' a three-hundred foot dam, Granny. It will flood the whole holler. They'll come in and buy us out or force us out — one or the other — and we'll have to move."

"They can't do that, can they?" said Granny. "Why, our family has been livin' on this creek for nigh-on two-hundred years. They can't just come in and flood us out."

"Oh, but I'm afraid they can," said Uncle Lawrence. When the government decides to do something, there's not too many things you can do to stop them."

164

"Do you mean," I asked, "they'll just come in and build a dam and flood us out?"

"No, Johnny," explained Dad, "they'll buy you out if you agree to their price. But if they want, they can just come in and take your land and house from you whether you like it or not."

That impressed me as a strange way for a government to do business — marchin' in and upsettin' everybody's life like that. It just didn't seem fair. I left the conversation at the dinner table and climbed the hillside behind Granny's place. Lookin' down, I could see my house, Granny's house, the fillin' station, and the other houses scattered along the creek. I tried to imagine it all bein' under water with ol' Be-elzebub, the devil catfish, swimmin' in and out of Granny's kitchen window. In my mind, it was a terrible sight. There was Eddie Brown, dressed in scuba gear, mannin' the gas pumps at the station, while Grit and Hodgekins wrestled a giant snappin' turtle. And there was the old graveyard, where Napoleon and Ezra and all of the other Kincaid clan were buried, grown over with lake weeds and pond scum. High above me on the surface of the lake, I saw Mom, Dad, and Granny treadin' water while a giant man-eatin' lake carp nibbled at their toes.

Suddenly I realized I was sittin' on the bottom, deep beneath the surface of the lake. The weight of the water was pressin' in against me. My lungs were screamin' out for air, and my eyes were bulgin' out in panic. My chest was about to bust, but I knew if I breathed in, my lungs would be filled with water. I rolled over on my back, strugglin' not to breath and tryin' desperately to figure a way out of my predicament. I fought as long as I could, but eventually my body forced me to breathe again. My mouth opened against my will, and I sucked in a long, deep, smotherin' breath of — air. I opened my eyes to see the white, puffy clouds

165

coastin'-by overhead. Sometimes, folks, my imagination goes off the deep end.

Boy, I thought, as I lay on dry ground with my breathin' gettin' easier and my heart poundin' less and less, I've gone from the rapture to the flood all in one day. I wondered what Biblical epic I'd be faced with tomorrow.

As I was lying there, I heard a cat meow. It sounded like Cleo. The sound came from the woods behind me. I jumped up and headed in the direction of the sound that lead me higher and deeper into the woods. I expect I spent the better part of an hour searchin' for that stupid cat, but when dusk set in, I had to return home empty-handed. The next day I added a two-dollar reward to my lost-cat poster at the fillin' station. But I never heard or saw Cleo again.

Over the next couple of months, the dam was the main topic of conversation on the creek. There were meetings. There were petitions. There were protests. There were speculations. But every bit of news seemed to bring that dam closer and closer to our doorstep.

Thinkin' about the dam was kinda like thinkin' about school in mid-June. I knew, come September, it would start up again, but I didn't want to think about it. Still, I'd find myself fishin' on the creek bank in the middle of summer when all the sudden, without warnin', the thought of school would flash across my mind. Try as I might to forget about it, I knew sooner or later the days would peter out, and summer would be over, and I'd be back in school again. What horrible thoughts plague a thirteen-year-old.

So, that's the way I thought about the dam — far away but comin' just as certain as the startin' of school in the fall. There was nothin' I could do to change or stop it, so I kept on pluggin' along as if it was never gonna happen. And yet, all along I knew someday that dam would be here and me and Mom and Granny — and all of Loop Creek — would

166

be gone and forgotten. Someday. But not today.

Then one day, like a thunderclap from an approachin' storm, the paper brought the official announcement. The dam would, indeed, be built on Loop Creek. We would have to move.

Shortly after the big announcement, Dad came home with more bad news. He called it good news. The company was openin' a new factory in North Carolina, and they wanted him to move down there to help set it up. Accordin' to Dad, it was an opportune time to move, especially since the government was gonna force us to move anyway. We might as well pack up and go to North Carolina. Me and Granny weren't too keen on the idea. We were well aware of the roots we had put down along this creek. Especially Granny. She had lived here for fifty years. I wondered how she would take to livin' somewhere else.

Talk about the comin' dam had everybody on the creek in an uproar, but somehow it didn't seem real to me. In fact, the first time that it really hit home was the day when Todd-n-Wilbur's truck pulled into the fillin' station. When it stopped at the pump, everybody's mouths dropped open. There was only one man in the truck. Now in all of my life, I had never seen Todd without Wilbur, or Wilbur without Todd. They always traveled and worked together. In my mind, they couldn't be separated. To tell you the truth, I wasn't sure which one it was sittin' in the truck and which one was missin'. Fortunately, Hodgekins knew.

"Hello, Todd-n-Wil — I mean Todd," said Hodgekins. "Where's your buddy Wilbur?"

"He's gone, Hodgekins," said Todd with a lost look on his face. "He's already sold out and moved to Mingo County. Didn't even stop to say good-bye."

It was then I knew we were all doomed. It was then I thought that maybe, just maybe, the rapture had come a couple of months ago, and only my cat Cleo had been taken home to heaven. The rest of us were certainly in the midst of great tribulation, just like the preacher had predicted. I went home to find a U-Haul in my yard. Dad had started to pack up, too.

I'll never forget my last night on Loop Creek. The movin' truck was nearly loaded, so Dad told me I could take a break. I went over to Granny's porch and joined her on the swing. Evenin' had come, but there was still enough light to silhouette the trees and mountains against the sky. Only the brightest stars had made their appearance. I wanted to talk to Granny, but she seemed far away in thought. She didn't notice me lovingly studyin' her face. She was sittin' quietly, lookin' at the mountains, smilin'. But it wasn't a happy smile. Then again, it wasn't necessarily a sad smile either. In fact, I don't think a word has been invented to describe what I saw on her face that night. It impressed me as a unique combination of melancholy, mixed with all the memories of happy family-times that had occurred right here on this porch — picnics and photo sessions, weddin' preparations and birth announcements, songfests and just plain family philosophizin'. All of that rememberin' seemed to be wrapped up in what I saw in her face that night, and I didn't want to interrupt her. At last, when the time seemed right for talkin', I posed a question for her. It just came out of my mouth. I've often wondered what prompted me to ask it.

"Granny, what do you suppose happened to Cleo?"

"Don't know, Johnny. Probably never will know." She paused and bit her lip. "You know, sometimes things just happen. Sometimes it comes time for things to pass on. And I guess it was just time for Cleo to pass on."

"But I still miss her, Granny."

"Oh, I know, son, I know. Sometimes pets and things

are loved just as much as humans — sometimes even more. And that's what makes it so hard sometimes tryin' to hold onto things. We get used to livin' a certain way. We get used to a certain set of friends and company. We get fond of a certain sunset, or the shape of a certain mountainside, the shade of certain tree. And after a while, we begin to believe we belong here. That somehow these mountains are our home. And that it's a place that will never change, a place we will never have to leave. But that will never happen in this world, son. There always will come a time for everything to pass on — even Loop Creek."

"But leavin' hurts, Granny. I got kinda used to these old mountains."

"I know, Johnny. When we have to leave something we love, it always will hurt. But what you — and me — got to do is have the grace and dignity to accept the passin' and have enough faith in the Good Lord to trust that He knows what He's doin'. Who knows, maybe someday we'll call North Carolina our home, too."

"Oh, I don't think so, Granny," I said, slowly shakin' my head.

"And why not?" she asked.

"'Cause we won't find any *magic* there like we have in *these* mountains, on *this* creek."

Granny patted me on my knee, sighed, and got up to walk over to the truck where Mom and Dad were standin'. About halfway down the porch steps, she turned, looked me straight in the eyes, and smiled that melancholy smile of hers. Her face was highlighted by the dim light shining out from the living room window. There were tears in her eyes. Her voice quivered as she spoke.

"You're right, boy. You're absolutely plum-right."

Then she turned and disappeared down the steps into the now darkened yard.

Books by John Kincaid

City Boy, Country Heart

"A meandering mosaic of misty mountain memories." A sentimental, humorous look at growing up in West Virginia in the early 1960s. Must reading for Baby Boomers and other children at heart.

My Loop Creek Country Friends

"A book you'll have to read barefoot." Tall tales and other true stories. Learn why West Virginians don't like wearing shoes and the good-news truth about cholesterol.

Mountain Yarns

Homespun stories woven from the threads of life.

Coming Soon: What I Learned in Sunday School

To Order: Send a copy of the form below to:
Kincaid Kountry Books,
105 Cherrywood Addition,
Scott Depot, WV 25560

Make checks payable to Kincaid Kountry Books

	Unit Price	Number	Total
City Boy, Country Heart	$6.00	____	_____
Loop Creek Country Friends	10.00	____	_____
Mountain Yarns	9.00	____	_____
WV sales tax, 6%			_____
Shipping and Handing			_Free!
		Total	_____